SARAH DIXON lives in Yo[...] two children. Her love of s[...] battle the Daleks. She now k[...] all times, just in case! After [...] sci-fi, her brain was so full of story ideas and memories of things her children had said or done that *Alfie Slider vs the Shape Shifter* came pouring out of her fingertips.

Sarah aims to write books that adults will enjoy reading to children as much as children enjoy reading themselves. Stories to bring families together, packed with action, adventure and a side order of humour.

Sarah's world(s) don't only revolve around Alfie Slider, and she also creates short stories for all ages. She has been included in a number of anthologies, has won an award for a ghost story and is a member of writing group York Writers. When she isn't writing Sarah can probably be found visiting a school somewhere, encouraging children to read, write or save the world!

For further information visit: www.sarahdixonwriter.com

To Gracie

ALFIE SLIDER
VS THE SHAPE SHIFTER

SARAH DIXON

Enjoy!
Sarah Dixon

SilverWood

Published in 2017 by SilverWood Books

SilverWood Books Ltd
14 Small Street, Bristol, BS1 1DE, United Kingdom
www.silverwoodbooks.co.uk

Copyright © Sarah Dixon 2017

The right of Sarah Dixon to be identified as the author of this work
has been asserted in accordance with the Copyright, Designs
and Patents Act 1988 Sections 77 and 78.

All rights reserved. No part of this publication may be reproduced,
stored in a retrieval system, or transmitted in any form or by any means,
electronic, mechanical, photocopying, recording or otherwise,
without prior permission of the copyright holder.

This is a work of fiction. Names, characters, places and incidents
either are products of the author's imagination or are used fictitiously.
Any resemblance to actual events or locales or persons,
living or dead, is entirely coincidental.

ISBN 978-1-78132-591-9 (paperback)
ISBN 978-1-78132-592-6 (ebook)

British Library Cataloguing in Publication Data
A CIP catalogue record for this book is available from
the British Library

Page design and typesetting by SilverWood Books
Printed on responsibly sourced paper

*For David, Aiden and Niamh, who make all things possible
Love you to space and back, in any universe*

One

'Warning! Warning! Shields failing. Ship's power at fifty-two per cent and falling.'

The captain of the spaceship sat, grim-faced, his hands moving lightning quick over the controls spread across the flight desk in front of him. Lights came on, or went off, in response to a flick of his finger.

'Computer,' he barked, 'status of this sector?'

The view screen that hung above the control panel showed a view of our galaxy that no one on Earth had ever seen; the view from the outside. Overlaying this image, a red light appeared and outlined our solar system.

'Technology in this system is emergent,' the computer stated. Its voice sounded like a calmer version of the captain's, making it seem like he was talking the problem through with himself, out loud.

'Well, we can't crash here then. Find me a parallel with a primitive status.'

'Searching...'

The entire ship rocked, the captain grabbed at the console before him to avoid being thrown across the bridge.

'Direct hit to starboard laser array. Sensors offline.

Situation critical,' the computer reported, matter-of-factly.

Muttering a curse under his breath, the captain sat back in his seat and pulled straps over both shoulders which he secured into a buckle that rose from the seat below.

'Parallel identified.'

'Do we have enough power for an FTL hop to that system and a TR shift?' the captain asked.

'Probability of success, eighty-seven per cent,' came the calm response.

'Close enough...' said the captain. His hands moved quickly over the console in front of him, turning off the blinking of some lights and switching others on in their place. The screen above him showed nearby stars and planets turning into streaks of light as the ship lurched forward at incredible speed.

'Initiating TR jump in five...four...three...two...one.'

The captain winced, throwing himself back into his seat and bracing his feet against the floor. For a few seconds his face wobbled and contorted like a blancmange in a washing machine, then he was still. He swallowed, pressing his lips tight and puffing out cheeks that had taken on a sickly green tinge.

'TR jump successful,' the computer said.

The view screen cleared to black for a moment, and then a view of a solar system appeared. A different solar system than before. Where Earth had been was a similar planet except the continents were in different places and they were grey-brown, not green. At the centre of the system were two yellow-red suns.

The captain grunted, his jaw still tight with tension. It was a moment or two and another hard swallow before he asked, 'No sign we're being followed?'

'No. However, sensors are at diminished capacity.'

'Status?'

The computer started listing the names of all the ship's systems and how well they were working. By the time it was done, the captain's shoulders had slumped downwards and he sat, shaking his head with a tired expression.

'I'm stuck here for now, and no way to even get a message back to HQ?' he asked, but he didn't wait for an answer from the computer. 'Tell me more about the emergent system we just jumped from.'

The view screen above the control panel cleared then showed an image of our solar system zooming quickly in to the planet Earth.

'This planet, known locally as Earth, is inhabited by the human race. They have developed space flight and have begun active exploration of their own solar system.'

'We'll need an access point. We need to monitor Earth for activity by those pirates. We can't let them expose Earth to advanced technology. Then we need to alert the Skolto Service to launch a rescue mission.'

'Agreed.'

The captain leaned back in his chair, chewing on his bottom lip as he viewed the image of Earth and the data about its people that was displayed underneath. His jaw was firm, his expression thoughtful. After a few minutes, his features relaxed into a smile, and he nodded his head in response to some thought he'd had.

'Alright. I think we can make this work. Computer, give me a list of repairs needed to open a TR access point. Let's get to work!'

Two

Alfie Slider skidded into the alley. His brain was busy making excuses to his mum for why he was late home; he knew she'd be worried. When the sound reached his ears it sent an urgent signal to his brain: stop. His arms and legs quickly did as they were told.

It had been a choking sort of sound. The sort of sound you make when you've put too much food in your mouth, Alfie thought, or you have something stuck in your throat. The sort of sound that would usually make him rush towards someone, to ask, 'Are you alright?'

But Alfie didn't rush, and he didn't ask. His throat felt itchy and too tight to speak. He'd run down this alley countless times. It was always a bit dark, especially where it turned the corner. It smelled of a weird mixture of paint, damp, and the cooking smells from people's houses, but Alfie had always felt safe here. Right now his belly was cold and all he could hear was his own loud breathing.

Someone or something made that noise, he thought, peering into the darkness. Nothing. Maybe they were around the corner. Alfie cautiously approached the turn and peeped around. Empty.

Shaking his head, Alfie wondered why, if there was nothing to see, the flickering sensation in his stomach was telling him that something was very, very, wrong.

Sensing movement behind him, in the deepest part of the shadows, Alfie quickly turned towards it. As he did, a flash of bright light down on the ground captured his gaze. Quicker than thought, Alfie bent down and picked the shining object up, flinching as it thrummed in his grasp.

Turning his palm up, he looked at the thing. At first he couldn't make it out; his eyes were struggling to focus... or was the thing moving? Changing? After blinking and really concentrating Alfie saw that it was a key. A really shiny key.

His hand closed around it as he pulled it into his chest. A scuttering sound behind him made Alfie whip his head around again. He stared into the darkness for a moment, then his feet took over. He ran down the alley and out towards the street beyond.

Like a lighthouse in a stormy sea, the street lamp at the end of the alley called Alfie to safety. His shoulders relaxed the moment he was inside the circle of light, sending his backpack sliding off the slope of his shoulder. For just a moment the lamplight caught the reflective logo: Green Hill School. Alfie pulled the strap back onto his shoulder and ran for home, tightly clutching the key.

Three

'You're late!' Alfie's mum's shout was triggered the moment he opened the front door. Alfie winced, trying to work out just how much trouble he was in. His mum sounded just a little bit annoyed, a tiny bit relieved, but mostly just pleased to see him. Alfie felt a smile tugging his lips upwards with relief.

Pausing just inside the door, Alfie took a moment to enjoy the feeling of coming home. The house was warm and smelled of clean laundry and cooking. It was easy to forget that creeping feeling of being watched from the alley. A big smile spread across his face as he walked into the kitchen.

'Sorry, Mum.'

'Hmmm.' Mum gave him a pretend glower. 'Don't be sorry, be on time,' she added a moment later.

Alfie knew that his mum never stayed cross for long, and sure enough, it was only a second later that she stepped forward to wrap him in a hug. He squeezed back, savouring the feeling of warmth and comfort. He might not want to do hugs in public these days, but that didn't mean he didn't enjoy them.

As she stepped back, Mum said, 'What's that you're clutching in your hand? Did you find The One Ring on your way home?' She lapsed into a bad Gollum impression, 'Myyyy preciousss!'

Alfie hadn't realized his fingers were still so tightly wrapped around the shiny key. Now Mum had mentioned it he knew it was a bit of a strange way to behave. He realized that a part of him wanted the attention turned away from him, from the key. He rolled his eyes and muttered, 'Geek.'

'Mmmhmm,' Mum agreed, comfortable with the label he'd given her. 'So, what is it?' She nodded her head towards his clenched fist.

Alfie frowned. He thought about opening his hand, but his fingers just didn't do as they were told. He realized he didn't want to show the key to anyone, not even Mum.

Looking up at her, he saw she was waiting, eyebrows raised, lines of concern deepening on her forehead.

Trying to keep his voice casual, Alfie said, 'A key. I found it in the alley.' He had to force his reluctant fingers to open. As they uncurled, the kitchen lights dimmed for a moment.

'Dodgy connection,' Mum muttered, distracted by the flicker. Returning her attention to the key she said, 'No key ring. Someone will be sorry they lost that.'

She started to put her hand out to touch it then paused with her fingers hovering above. There was a worried wrinkle in her brow, as though there was something about the key that unsettled her. After a moment she flexed her fingers and turned away to the cooker.

'Dad will be home in ten minutes, get changed? Pizza tonight.'

Alfie nodded, shoulders slumping in relief that the key was still safe in his hand. He kept quiet, worried that the tone of his voice would make his mum realize something odd was happening. Turning to walk out of the kitchen, he thought, I need to get a really good look at this key.

His mum's voice brought him to a halt, 'Make a poster.'

'Hmmm?' Alfie asked, looking back over his shoulder.

'For the key,' Mum explained. 'So we can find who lost it.'

Alfie paused, swallowed and then nodded. Just the suggestion of someone else having the key was making him feel queasy, but he couldn't understand why he felt that way.

Why should he care so much about a key? He didn't even know what it opened. Still, his hand was wrapped around it again as he went upstairs to change.

Four

Alfie waited until after dinner to have a really good look at the key. Dad was giving his sister, Lizzie, a bath. He could hear Mum moving around in the kitchen downstairs so he knew that he had some time where he wouldn't be disturbed. Sitting cross-legged on his bed, he lay the key down on the duvet and inspected it.

It was unusually shiny, not just like a new key might be, but like a piece of jewellery or the chrome on the vintage cars his grandad had taken him to see last summer. It looked polished. Shape and size were just what you would expect a key to be, the kind you use in a front door that has a round end and a bar sticking out of it with zigzag teeth. There was nothing written on it, no brand name or serial number or anything that might tell him more about it.

Alfie picked it up to turn it over, the other side was just as plain as the first but as he held it, he realized something else. The key was really heavy. Scrambling off the bed, he started rummaging in drawers in his desk. He knew that he had another key in there somewhere. Alfie had kept one of the keys to their old house when they'd moved to remind him of the old house. There had been happy memories there.

When he had both keys, Alfie put one in each hand and weighed them up against each other. The shiny key was definitely a lot heavier than the other one.

Alfie had an idea that how heavy a piece of metal was could tell you what it was made of, atomic weights or something, but he didn't know how to work it out. He could use the computer to search for the answer, but someone was bound to ask him questions about what he was doing. How could he explain how this key made him feel?

Well, Mum, he thought, I found this key and since then I don't want to put it down. I don't want anyone else to know about it, or touch it. It feels like it belongs to me. Yes, he could see that going down well.

Holding the shiny key up, he let it catch the light, watching the way it gleamed. He gasped as he realized what was so strange about it. The key didn't reflect anything but the light. There was no image of Alfie's room in the metal, no image of him!

Throwing the key down on the bed, Alfie stuffed his hands under his armpits. He didn't want to hold it anymore. How was that possible? Alfie knew how reflections worked, and he knew that you were supposed to see what was around you, only back to front. Upside down sometimes, too, like in spoons and spheres, but you should definitely see *something*. If you couldn't, wasn't that against the laws of physics?

What kind of metal didn't show proper reflections? Alfie imagined, for a moment, that he had found something magical. The key to the castle at Camelot, or to Merlin's spell book. The key didn't look ancient or magical, though; it looked modern. It looked brand new.

If it wasn't magic, then could it be a new invention? Had a spy dropped it when they were on a top-secret mission? Was this some amazing new technology, a super key that would open anything? That seemed a bit more likely but what would a spy be doing in an alley in the middle of a housing estate?

One thing Alfie was absolutely certain about was that it wasn't an ordinary key. He knew it, somehow, but he had no idea why. It wasn't just an ordinary house key that someone had lost. This key was going to lead him to something amazing.

Chewing his lip as he thought, Alfie shot off the bed again to pull something else out from his desk drawers. A microscope. It had been a Christmas gift when he was about seven, and Alfie hoped that the batteries still had some charge in them. He flicked the switch and the light came on.

Setting the microscope up on the bed, Alfie knelt down beside it and slid the key into the slot for specimens. His stomach buzzed with anticipation, like he was about to make an amazing discovery. Cautiously, he peered down the lens of the scope, moving the key around underneath the circle of light so he could inspect it all over.

There was nothing! Alfie felt the excitement leaking out of him and he sat back on his heels and sighed.

When the thought came, it came like they often did for Alfie, super quick. He knew that he knew something before he knew what it was. It was like his brain worked so quickly that the voice in his head couldn't keep up. Shaking his head, Alfie forced himself to calm down and let the thoughts come slowly.

There was nothing. Nothing. No fingerprints. No scratches. No machine marks from where the key had been cut. No speck of oil or dirt. Not one single imperfection on the whole of the key. That wasn't possible.

Alfie remembered all those times when he'd made a mistake and Mum had been trying to reassure him. She'd told him lots of times that there was no such thing as perfect, that everyone made mistakes, that nothing was ever exactly how it was planned. This key was, though.

Staring at the key for a few moments more, Alfie felt more and more uneasy. Picking it up, he put it carefully into the little silver train he'd been given when he was a baby and closed the lid. There was nothing more that Alfie could do to explain the mystery tonight. Maybe he'd think of something in the morning, after a good night's sleep.

Five

The moment his alarm went off Alfie sat up, eyes wide open and ready for the new day. Normally the first thing on his mind was whether it was a weekday or the weekend. Today his first thought was, Where is the key?

Heart thudding, Alfie rolled out of bed and rushed to the shelves where he had left it. It was safe and sound, still tucked inside the silver train.

The tightness in his stomach disappeared as Alfie grabbed the key and stared at it on his palm for a few seconds. Somehow, after a good night's sleep, it didn't seem so strange or worrying. It was just a key, after all.

Laying it carefully on his bed, he kept an eye on it while he got dressed, then he stuffed it deep into the pocket of his school trousers for safekeeping.

Alfie wasn't sure what to do next to learn more about it. One person who could always help him when he got stuck was his best friend, Amy. He thought that if he could get her somewhere quiet, at school, he might talk to her about the key.

Across the landing he could hear his Mum trying to wake his little sister, Lizzie, up. Lizzie wasn't a morning person at all. She was almost four, and when she was awake Mum described her as 'perpetual motion', but she was a slow starter.

Alfie helped out the way he did most mornings, poking his head around her bedroom door and calling, 'Hey, Lizzie, want to play a game?'

That worked. All three of them were soon downstairs, going about the normal morning routine. Breakfast, making lunches, and checking they had everything they needed for the day ahead. The only difference today was the weight of the key in Alfie's pocket, and a nervous and excited feeling whenever he thought of it.

It wasn't that odd things never happened to Alfie. His family didn't really do routine, so every day was different. Weekends were either spent doing sci-fi things for Mum, or having outdoor adventures with Dad. The odd was his routine, in a way. He didn't mind – he wasn't really a routine person either.

Other kids had told Alfie that he acted a bit weird, but like his parents always said, weird was just another word for different, and different was good. If everyone was the same, nothing would ever change. The key was a completely different kind of odd, though.

It was still tucked into his pocket as he walked to school. Mum and Lizzie were walking the same way to take Liz to pre-school. As they got near to the alley where he had found the key, Alfie's stomach writhed like he'd swallowed an electric eel.

Glancing sideways at Mum and Lizzie he saw that they were just walking along, like this was any other day. When they got near the corner, Lizzie asked to play with

Mum's keys. She asked to play with Mum's keys a lot, but when she asked today, Alfie's brain did a Mexican wave to get his attention.

Alfie watched as Mum handed over her keys with a smile, and Lizzie's chubby little hand fastened around them carefully. She knew she had to keep tight hold of them.

Alfie couldn't take his eyes off his sister as she tottered over to the fence, her forehead screwed up and eyes narrowed. She wasn't just looking at the fence; she was looking for something in particular.

Rushing over to get a closer look at what she was doing, Alfie was just in time to see Lizzie poke Mum's key into a scratch on the fence and give it a turn. Her face screwed up, grumpy, when nothing happened. Lower lip jutting out in a sulk, she pulled the key back and trotted on, looking for somewhere else to try.

Alfie took a step closer to the fence, trying to look casual. As he got nearer, the key started to buzz in his pocket like an angry bee. His hand reached in and closed around it just as he peered into a large knothole.

The breath rushed out of Alfie in surprise and reflex made him pull back. He had to check again, had he really seen that? He had. Inside the knothole was a shimmering, golden light.

If this was a video game that would be a secret level, he thought. He knew, he just *knew*, that if he put the key in there something amazing would happen.

'Alfie! Come on!' Mum's impatient shout pulled him back to reality. Releasing the key back into his pocket, Alfie took a step back, then turned and ran after his mum. He had the school day to get through but when he walked home, alone, he was going to test his theory.

Six

The hands on the clock moved painfully slowly through the hours of the school day. Most parents' evenings, Alfie's teachers would tell his mum and dad that he had a problem with focus. The humdrum of learning someone else's ideas was boring, and Alfie tended to get lost in his own thoughts. Today, when he had so much to think about, it was especially hard.

Alfie had been happily daydreaming about using the key and getting sucked into his favourite video game. He was just about to defeat the boss level, when an angry voice calling, 'Alfie Slider!' snapped him back to reality.

Alfie suspected from Miss Beavis' face and the silence from the rest of the class that it wasn't the first time she'd called his name. He was the centre of attention just when he least wanted to be.

'Alfie, I'm having to say your name too often. It's disrupting everyone else's learning. Get yourself to Mr Sloan's office, please,' Miss Beavis said in a tight, cross voice. Alfie winced and nodded, hoping he could show from his expression just how sorry he was.

'Mr Sloan isn't in today,' said Mrs Mahoney, the

teaching assistant. Miss Beavis blinked slowly, surprise registering on her face. Alfie felt the same way. Mr Sloan was *always* in school. People joked that he lived there.

Luckily for Alfie, Miss Beavis was so distracted that she just waved him back into his seat and went to whisper with Mrs Mahoney about the absent headmaster. Result! Alfie promised himself he'd pay more attention for the rest of the day.

As soon as the bell rang, Alfie was off like a shot. He grabbed his coat and bag from his locker and was first in the queue to leave. He could hear Amy calling his name behind him, but he pretended that he couldn't. He wanted to try out his idea with the knothole, and he didn't want *anyone* watching if he turned out to be wrong.

As soon as the door opened he was off, like a greyhound let off its lead. He zigzagged around the other kids, jumped over a ball that ran into his path, and then he was out the gate and running as fast as he could to the alley.

His mind was a whirl of excitement all the way there. Common sense told him that he was going to look like an idiot, shoving a key into a fence, but he felt so sure it was more than that. This didn't feel like normal life; it felt like he'd got caught up in in the plot of a film.

Alfie paused, took a deep breath and then tilted his head so he could see into the knothole. His stomach fizzed as he saw the same shimmering gold light.

The key started to vibrate in his pocket. As Alfie pulled it out, it felt like it was being tugged towards the knothole. It was like the key and the knothole were magnets that wanted to snap against each other.

That common sense part of his brain whispered, 'You're going to look like a right idiot...' and the other part said, 'This is going to be epic!' Neither part of his brain was prepared for what actually happened, though.

The key broke through the shimmering, golden light. Alfie felt like he was being blasted with warm air from all sides. The hair on his head stood on end and his whole body felt like it was being tickled by tiny fingers. The key was shaking so strongly that he was worried it would fly out of his grip. He grabbed it with the other hand too.

As the tingly, windy sensation grew in intensity, Alfie took a deep breath and held it. Just when he thought he would be blown away, the exact opposite happened. Pressure started at his scalp, tightening around him as though he was being pulled into an invisible tube. The pressure grew, the golden light got bigger and bigger as he was pulled towards it.

Alfie screamed.

Seven

Alfie hadn't known what to expect once he'd used the key, but the rushing, tingly feeling had felt like he was moving. Fast. He'd braced himself to land hard. But there was no hard impact, no crash – he was just standing in a different place.

It didn't feel at all like the alley any more. There was no wind, no birdsong or traffic noise, so he must be inside somewhere. There was a smell that seemed familiar, and Alfie tried to remember what it was. Then a memory popped into his head. Christmas morning, opening the robot kit he'd been waiting for. The smell was plastic, electronics and grease. An engine?

'Hello?' he called out into the darkness. Alfie wasn't sure if it would be better or worse to get an answer. He almost jumped out of his skin when, instead of a voice, there was a low whirr and a few moments later lights flickered on at floor level.

The lights ran around the outside of the wall, and Alfie soon realized they were marking out a half circle shape. The floor was black and rubbery, and as the space brightened they showed the walls curved overhead.

Alfie realized that he must be under a dome of some sort. The light revealed pipes and cables that criss-crossed the rounded walls, all heading towards a space exactly opposite where Alfie stood.

There was a soft, electrical click and a large rectangle began to glow in the middle of that space. Green characters that Alfie didn't recognize ran across what must be a large screen. A robotic-sounding voice said, 'Initializing…'

'Initializing what?' Alfie asked, looking around him as the lights revealed more of the space he was in. No answer.

The voice had sounded flat, like it was coming out of speakers, not from a person. Alfie hadn't noticed any sign of another person being here, but was someone watching him? There were so many odd looking bits of electronics sticking out of the walls it was possible, he couldn't tell if any of them might be cameras.

As the room brightened Alfie realized he was standing on a red circle painted on the floor. Turning on the spot to see the whole space, he discovered a doorway right behind him. It was set into the only straight wall in the room. There must be another room through there, he thought.

More lights flicked on, revealing a console underneath the screen. It was lit in red, green and yellow lights that illuminated dozens of switches and dials. There was a large swivel chair set in front of it.

Realizing he still held the key, Alfie glanced at it but it didn't look any different. He had half expected it to be gone, or to have changed somehow. He shoved it into his pocket.

'Initializing…' came the voice again.

As he stared around the room, Alfie felt an idea

growing in his mind. He tried to tell himself that it couldn't be right, that it was ridiculous. It made no sense. Or did it? The key was made from something he'd never seen before, something that defied the laws of physics.

The more he looked, the more he realized this scene was familiar, but he knew he'd never been here before. It was high tech. Everything was strange but it looked like it all had purpose, even if he wasn't sure what that was. It was like a set from one of his mum's sci-fi shows. Curved walls, control panel, view screen, pilot's seat. Alfie found the words coming out of his mouth in spite of the fact he knew it was impossible.

'I'm on a flying saucer!'

Eight

'System initialized. How would you like to be addressed?'

Alfie jumped, startled by the mechanical voice.

'Addressed?' Alfie cleared his throat, 'Ummm. I'm Alfie. Alfie Slider.'

'Acknowledged. Preliminary analysis identifies you as "human". Is this correct?'

What! What else could he be? Was this a joke or something? Was someone playing a trick on him?

'Yes, I'm human,' Alfie thought that was a safe reply. It wouldn't make him look like an idiot if this turned out to be a hidden-camera show. 'Who are you? Where am I?'

At exactly the same time as he spoke, the robot voice came again, 'Setting system preferences to human, please wait.'

Alfie watched as the bizarre symbols that had been moving across the screen changed into the familiar letters of the alphabet. Words were formed, some of them made sense but a lot of them didn't. Alfie had downloaded enough games onto his console to know what they were: installation messages.

Alfie read them, looking for any clues to answer his

questions. The words scrolled quickly, and he just had time to read familiar words like "system" and "profile". The text was moving too fast for him to read and make sense of the words he wasn't sure of.

Walking closer to the screen as he read, almost without thinking, Alfie sat down in the pilot's chair and gazed in wonder at the console. A disbelieving laugh bubbled up. If this was a joke, someone had gone to a lot of trouble.

Another voice spoke, Alfie let out a squeak of surprise. It wasn't the robotic voice from before. This one sounded human but it was still coming over the speakers.

'System preferences set.'

It was a nice voice, Alfie thought. A man's voice, a friendly one. Warmth and humour were in every word. It was a voice you could confide in. It sounded like the sort of voice you hear on the telly, announcing the next programme.

The screen cleared and showed a rotating image of a figure. Blond spiky hair, green eyes, school bag slung over one shoulder. It took him longer than it should have done, but with a start Alfie realized it was him! From the bug-eyed, slack-jawed expression Alfie decided it must have been taken just as he transported on board.

'Welcome on board the *Monkesto*, Alfie Slider. You are now recognized as this vessel's operator.'

Alfie was so caught up with what was happening on the display that it took him a few moments to realize that the system had lapsed into silence.

'Umm. Thank you? But, what is the *Monkesto*? *Where* is it?'

'The *Monkesto* is a spacefaring vessel, owned and operated by the Skolto Service. In Earth terms it is a secure transport. Earth technology has not advanced enough to describe its location accurately. My best attempt at translation is "stuck in a parallel universe",' the friendly voice explained.

Alfie's stomach rolled and he leaned back into the chair. A parallel universe? Alfie had heard that phrase before. He was pretty sure parallel universes were a sci-fi thing. He'd heard the term in episodes of *Star Trek* or *Doctor Who* that he'd watched with his mum. That wasn't the part that he couldn't stop thinking about though. It was the other word. Stuck.

'What do you mean, stuck?' Alfie asked, not quite able to keep a squeaky tone of panic from his voice.

'The *Monkesto* is currently incapable of flight, or trans-reality shifts.'

Alfie felt like he was getting a headache. His brain was throbbing inside his skull.

'Can I get home?' he asked. The simple question had become the most important thing to him.

'Of course!' the voice was full of reassurance. 'The *Monkesto* can be voice operated. Simply move to the transport hub and request "Return".'

Alfie thought about that for a moment. He was burning with questions, and a big part of him wanted to ask them. A bigger part wanted to make sure that he could get back home first.

'Can I come back here again, if I leave?'

'Of course!' the voice spoke those words in exactly the same way, reminding Alfie he was talking to a machine.

'Return is possible via the access point.'

Every answer that came from the voice brought more questions. Alfie took a breath, let it out and tried to do what his teachers were always telling him to: focus.

'I'm going to go back then.'

There was no reply.

Sliding off the seat, Alfie looked around in search of the transport hub. A spotlight helpfully flicked on over the red circle that he had been standing on when he arrived. Alfie walked towards it, braced himself and then said, 'Ret...' he stopped, realizing something.

'Ummm, what do I call you?' he asked the voice.

'I am the ship's computer. I have no need of a name unless you wish me to have one.'

Alfie thought about that, then decided it would feel rude not to have a name for such a nice voice.

'Mr Monk. Mr Monk of the *Monkesto*.'

'System preferences updated,' was the only reply.

Alfie nodded, happy with that, 'Alright. Return.'

No sooner had he spoken than that sense of being in a wind tunnel started.

Alfie closed his eyes as pressure built in his scalp, and he felt like he was being sucked up into a giant straw. Just seconds later and the blasts of air stopped and he could hear familiar noises, cars in the distance, dogs barking, birds singing.

Smiling, he opened his eyes to find himself back in the alleyway. Alfie let out a cry of triumph. He couldn't believe it. He'd been to a parallel universe and back!

He punched the air to let out a bit of the excitement but was quickly reaching into his pocket for the key again.

He had so many questions. He couldn't wait to get back to the ship and ask them.

Key in hand, Alfie walked towards the knothole again, preparing himself for the weird transport sensation. Just as the key started vibrating, just as he was about to put it into the knothole, a loud beeping sound from his wrist pulled him back. His alarm!

Checking his watch, Alfie growled in frustration. It was time to go home. He looked from the key to the watch and back again, debating, then sighed heavily. It was Friday night, so tomorrow was the weekend. He'd have plenty of time to ask his questions then. If he stayed now and upset his parents, he might not be allowed out at the weekend at all. He reluctantly decided it was better to wait.

Alfie felt frustration making his limbs stiff and heavy but, as he started running back towards his house, he couldn't help but laugh. No one was going to believe this!

Nine

Alfie burst through the front door, leaving it wide open as he ran into the kitchen.

'Mum! You'll never guess...'

'Were you born in a barn? Shut the door, Alfie!' Mum's voice cut him off like a splash of cold water to the face. It broke the spell a bit. There was nothing more normal than being nagged by your mum.

'Good day at school?' she asked, raising her voice a bit so it would reach him in the hall.

Alfie took the hint and went back to shut the door, grinning.

'Yes, OK I suppose.'

His mum was waiting for him when he was done, arms open for a welcoming hug. As she got nearer, something she saw made her stop and pull back to look at his face more closely.

'Not just OK! You've had a great day. I can tell. You look all excited about something.' His smile was making her smile too. 'Will you tell me about it later? When Lizzie is asleep so I can listen properly?'

Alfie had wanted to tell Mum everything, right then

and there, but he liked the idea of talking to her later. Lizzie was famous for her interruptions.

Alfie remembered the time she'd walked in while he was trying to tell Mum about something serious that had happened at school. They'd been concentrating on each other and hadn't realized until she started singing, 'I'm doing the naked dance!' that she had stripped and was wiggling her bare bottom at them. Lizzie was always a mix of funny and frustrating, perhaps talking later would be better.

'Yes please,' Alfie said. Mum made it a promise with a kiss to the top of his head.

It wasn't until after Dad was home, they'd eaten diner, done homework and got ready for bed that Alfie had a chance to talk to his parents. Mum came downstairs after putting Lizzie to bed, sat down in the armchair with a sigh and turned to Alfie.

'Alright, your turn! Tell me what happened today.'

Dad looked up from his tablet computer, 'Oh, something happened?' He clicked the off switch, put the tablet down and got ready to listen.

Alfie savoured the moment. It wasn't often he got his mum and dad all to himself like this. He found it hard to know where to start, though.

'Umm,' he began. Then he felt the key pressing into his leg from the pocket of his trousers and realized where he needed to start, 'You know I found that key?'

His parents nodded.

'Well, I found where it goes. There's an access point, in the alley.'

Mum's forehead wrinkled, her eyebrows lifted up in

silent surprise. Alfie went on, the words rushing out of him now he was finally getting to tell someone.

'When you put the key in, you end up somewhere else. A parallel universe. How could that happen?'

'Oh!' Mum frowned for a moment as she thought about it. 'Well, some sci-fi shows have transporters that can beam you from one place to another. They break you down into atoms, store your "pattern" in the ship's transport system and then put you back together on the other side. Other shows have portals. You just step through those to get somewhere else. They're sort of folds and holes in the fabric of space-time. There's always magic, of course, but when you say access point that sounds like you're thinking sci-fi?'

'Umm, yes, I suppose,' Alfie replied, a bit distracted by the idea that his atoms had been pulled apart and put back together. 'I was transported to a spaceship that was stuck in a parallel universe. It must be alien, because the system had to be reset to human. I can go back any time I want!'

Alfie felt his shoulders loosening with the relief of telling something the whole story. He looked expectantly at his parents, first Mum, then Dad, eager to see their reaction.

'Great start, Alfie!' Dad was the first to reply, and Mum nodded quickly in agreement.

'Yes, great start. Write it down before you forget it?'

Alfie blinked, disappointment settling over him like a heavy blanket. They thought he was just talking about writing a story!

'Nice touch. The system reset.' Dad added.

'So what's the rest of the plot? Do you have to repair the spaceship, or are you going to explore the parallel universe?' Mum asked.

'I don't know.' A sulky tone crept into Alfie's voice.

Mum's eyebrows lifted in question again, and Alfie realized that he had a choice to make. He could either try and convince them that this was real, or play along that it was just a story. If he convinced them, they'd probably take the key away and give it to the authorities. If they did that, Alfie would never get the answers to all his questions.

He took a deep breath and told his first lie.

'I think I need to do a bit more research before I decide what happens next in the story.'

Mum and Dad nodded in agreement. Alfie kissed them both goodnight and ran upstairs to think.

Ten

Alfie woke early the next morning, with no need for an alarm. As soon as he remembered what he was doing that day, he got a huge burst of energy, as if he'd drunk one of those cans of energy drink. He jumped out of bed, grabbed the clothes that he'd laid out on the bed the night before and dressed quickly.

Creeping quietly out of his room, Alfie peered into the other bedrooms. Mum and Lizzie were still asleep but there was no sign of Dad. When Alfie got downstairs he spotted the note by the kettle, "Gone for a run, back about nine."

Alfie felt a smile creeping over his face as the butterflies in his stomach disappeared with a sigh. He'd been worried that he wouldn't be able to keep his secret this morning. He felt like he was buzzing all over. There was no way he could hide his feelings from his parents. He knew if anyone asked him, he would just blurt it all out. If he didn't have to talk to anyone, that was perfect.

As he packed a backpack with snacks and drinks, he thought about what he was going to ask Mr Monk today. He didn't want to waste a moment of his time. He had so many questions to ask, he just hoped that he would understand the answers.

Alfie was still lost in thought when he jogged into the alley, his hand reaching into his pocket for the key. He was nearing the corner when a noise up ahead caught his attention. He wasn't the only person in the alley.

Slowing down, Alfie ran his fingers through his hair, trying to look casual. He was just a kid, out for a walk in the early morning. Nothing to see here.

The morning sunlight hadn't got as far as the corner of the alley, which made it hard to see any detail. Peering into the gloom, he could just make out a figure, standing right by the knothole. It looked a bit hunched over, or, a nasty thought whispered to Alfie, maybe that's just what shape they normally were.

Alfie went cold all over. Was this who actually owned the key? An alien? Clenching his fists, Alfie summoned all his courage. He needed to find out what was going on. As he took a step closer and his eyes adjusted to the light, he realized that the figure didn't look strange at all. In fact, the tall shape was familiar. That wasn't an alien – that was his headmaster!

'Oh! Good morning, Mr Sloan,' Alfie said, covering up his surprise by giving his headmaster a respectful nod.

The teacher didn't even look up, he just made a sort of grunting noise and carried on staring at the ground. That was unusual, Alfie thought. Mr Sloan was strict, sure, but he could also be a lot of fun and he was usually friendly. It didn't seem like he was in a friendly mood today, though.

Unsure of what to do next, Alfie decided the best thing

was to keep walking. He didn't want to draw attention to the knothole or the key that felt heavy in his pocket.

Sidling past Mr Sloan, Alfie kept going until he was out of the alley. He didn't really have a plan for where to go; he just knew he had to get away from the alley and give himself some time to think.

Why was Mr Sloan stood just there? Was it a coincidence? Did the key *belong* to Mr Sloan?

No, that didn't make sense. The system had reset to human. Unless…was Mr Sloan an alien?

Thoughts tumbled round and round in Alfie's head. Maybe Mr Sloan had just been out for a walk. Alfie thought he lived around here. Maybe he'd just dropped something and was distracted. There had to be an explanation but which was it, the normal or the alien?

There was only one way to know for sure, Alfie decided. He needed to get back to the alley. As he walked in a loop, taking him away from the alley and then back again, Alfie came up with a plan. If Mr Sloan was still there, he would walk right up to him and ask if he needed any help. One way or another, that should sort things out.

Alfie practised asking casually in his head as he walked. His stomach churned as he got near to the alley. Stopping just out of sight of the entrance, he peered around the fence before he showed himself. It was empty.

Relief washed over Alfie like a cool breeze. Talking to your headmaster was nerve wracking enough, but talking to your headmaster when you think they might be an alien? That's something else altogether.

Alfie did a quick check around the corner to make sure that was clear too, he didn't want anyone to see him using the key. He didn't know what it would look like to someone watching, but if someone saw him just disappearing from the alley, they'd be bound to call the police or something.

With his checking completed, Alfie took a deep breath and ran to the knothole, shoved in the key and whoosh! This time his face was split with a wide grin as he was rushed away to the *Monkesto*.

He arrived in exactly the same spot as last time. Nothing seemed to have changed since he left. The lights came on and the system whirred into life, the same status messages scrolling over the screen.

'Hello, Mr Monk!' Alfie called cheerfully.

There was no reply.

Alfie sat down in the chair, wondering why the computer hadn't answered. Was it not working today? 'Mr Monk?'

'That is not a complete question, Alfie Slider,' was the odd reply, in that TV-friendly voice.

Alfie slapped himself on the forehead with the palm of his hand. What an idiot! He needed to remember he was talking to a computer, not a person. It would answer questions, but you had to ask them first, and it didn't need you to use nice manners.

'Does the *Monkesto* belong to Mr Sloan?'

'The *Monkesto* is owned and operated by the Skolto Service,' Mr Monk replied.

Alfie thought about that. 'Does Mr Sloan work for the Skolto Service?' he tried.

'One moment. Cross-checking employment files,' Mr Monk said cheerfully, adding just seconds later, 'No, there is no Mr Sloan on file as an employee of the Skolto Service.'

'So, who dropped the key?' Alfie asked, pulling it from his pocket and putting it down on the console.

A light appeared, shone on it, and seconds later a picture of the key appeared on the screen.

'The device you refer to as "the key" was previously locked to Captain Venka.'

Alfie swallowed around a lump that had appeared in his throat.

'Captain Venka is no longer the operator of this vessel. Controls are now biologically linked to you, Alfie Slider.'

Alfie chewed his lip as he thought about that. He had no idea what the computer meant. Every answer he got left him wanting to ask ten more. This was going to be a long day.

'Where is Captain Venka?' he asked, narrowing his eyes as he waited for the answer.

'Captain Venka's whereabouts are unknown. His vital signs were last detected thirty-nine hours and fifteen minutes ago at these coordinates.' As the computer spoke, the display screen was filled with the bright colours of a map.

Alfie realized with a start that it was a map of the streets near his home. The flashing light was right on the spot where he had found the key.

'How did you lose his...' Alfie tried to remember the words, '...vital signs?'

'There are a number of possibilities,' Mr Monk replied. 'Captain Venka may have been moved to a location outside this vessel's scanning abilities, or his vital signs may have ceased.'

A sour feeling started in Alfie's belly.

'You mean…he might be dead?'

'It is possible,' Mr Monk replied then went on, 'Additional life signs were in the location at the time.'

'Whose?' Alfie was sitting forward now, his heart thumping.

Two further dots appeared on the screen. One, Alfie realized was his own, just entering the alley. The other was in the corner, right by where he'd found the key. Right where he'd felt like he was being watched. 'That's me and…who?' Alfie asked.

'The identity of the other being is unknown. Scans suggest he was of the Variado race.'

Mr Monk paused, and Alfie thought he was going to stop there, but he didn't.

The screen cleared and the map was replaced with a picture of a dark shadow or cloud of goo. A black, shapeless thing.

'The Variado are a race of shape-changers. This is their unformed state but they can look like any being, or any thing,' Mr Monk explained.

Alfie felt like an icy breeze was blowing on his neck, all the hairs on his arms stood on end.

'Why would a Variado be there, in the alley, with Captain Venka?'

'The Variado are, in Earth terms, pirates,' Mr Monk replied, 'They are known for raiding vessels and taking their cargo.'

'Cargo?' Alfie asked, his voice thin and worried.

'The *Monkesto* currently carries two items of cargo, to be delivered to the Skolto Service Headquarters. One is a shipment of Fajiro frogs. The contents of the second crate are not available to this vessel's system or its operator.'

Alfie shook his head. He couldn't believe what he was hearing. He'd thought he was going to spend an exciting day exploring a spaceship, not walk into this sort of trouble!

The captain had disappeared, and there was a shape-changing alien after the ship or the cargo. What was Alfie supposed to do about that?

Eleven

Pulling his drinks bottle from his backpack, Alfie took a swig of water and decided to change tactics. There were other things that he needed to learn more about.

'You said the *Monkesto* is stuck in a parallel universe. How did it get there?'

'Captain Venka issued the order to make a trans-reality jump,' Mr Monk replied.

Alfie made a frustrated noise, then tried to cover it by loudly clearing his throat. That wasn't an answer! Was the computer trying to hide something?

'Why?'

'The *Monkesto* had sustained damaged. It was unable to return to a safe region of space, or make contact with the Skolto Service to arrange rescue. Captain Venka made the decision to hide the *Monkesto* in a parallel universe for two reasons: to secure the cargo and to prevent the primitive human society from accessing this vessel and its technology.'

Alfie listened to the computers reply carefully. There was a lot he didn't really understand in what Mr Monk was saying. Worse than that, from the moment Mr

Monk said one particular word, Alfie's stomach had clenched in anger.

'We're not primitive! We've invented loads of things. Why couldn't we see this technology? It's amazing! If our scientists could see all this, they could do so much to help the planet. We have problems! Dirty air and people dying of diseases and stuff. You can't keep it to yourselves!'

Mr Monk's voice was as pleasant and patient as ever as it replied to Alfie, 'Experience has shown that when relatively primitive societies are given access to advanced technologies, the results are unpredictable. Following the complete destruction of the planet Milito, it was forbidden to share advanced technology for safety reasons.'

Alfie could still feel the anger rumbling around inside him like thunder. He didn't much like being called primitive! He remembered how proud he'd felt of the human race when he'd visited the National Space Centre. He'd stood at the bottom of the Blue Streak rocket, looking all the way up at something that had actually been into space! People were amazing!

Then a little nagging feeling started in his brain, and he remembered some of the things his parents talked about. They worried about how much money was spent on weapons when people were sick or hungry. Alfie shifted in his seat as he began to suspect that Mr Monk might be right.

Swigging down some more water from his bottle, Alfie washed it around his mouth noisily. He swallowed, deciding to leave that tricky subject for now and go back to something that was probably more important anyway.

'How did the *Monkesto* get damaged?'

'The *Monkesto* came under fire from another vessel.'

'The Variano?' Alfie guessed.

'*Variado*,' Mr Monk corrected. 'That is the most likely scenario. Sensor readings at the time were consistent with an energy weapon used by the Variado.'

'The Skolto Service doesn't know the ship is here?' Alfie checked.

'That is correct. Communications systems are offline.'

'Does anything work on this ship?' Alfie asked with a hint of sarcasm.

'Life support is fully functional. Captain Venka made some repairs to transportation but the system is still limited. Scanners are limited, but the ship's system has been wired into the Earth internet. Combat systems are in need of repair.'

'So, what are we supposed to do about that?' Alfie asked.

'The safest course of action would be to do nothing,' the computer replied.

'There's a Variado out there, looking for the key!' Alfie protested.

'It does not know *you* have the key, or it would have already tried to take it. A Variado is motivated by profit. When it realizes it cannot find the key or the ship, it will probably just leave.'

'Probably?'

'Statistically, it is the most likely scenario. In time, the Skolto Service will locate this vessel. Until then the *Monkesto* is as secure as it can be.'

Alfie hummed to himself, squinting as he thought about it. He supposed it made sense, and Mr Monk certainly knew more about all of this than he did.

'So, how many alien races are there, then?' Alfie asked.

'Due to the developmental status of the Human Race, any information about other worlds and races is only available on a need to know basis,' Mr Monk replied.

'I'm the operator of a spaceship. I need to know!' Alfie protested.

'Further alien encounters are unlikely. There is no need to expose you to potentially harmful knowledge about alien technology or civilizations.'

Alfie's eyebrows met in the middle, he was frowning so deeply. 'So, you want me to help you, but you won't tell me anything I need to know?'

'Incorrect, Alfie Slider. I will tell you anything you *need* to know.'

Alfie let out an exasperated breath and rummaged in his bag for another snack. There had to be questions that he could get the answers to, if he could just work out which ones to ask.

Twelve

Time whizzed past at light speed, Alfie had so many questions for the computer. He didn't always get answers, but he certainly got a lot to think about. When he went home to have dinner with his family, he couldn't stop thinking about the *Monkesto*, the Variado and how he was probably the only person who knew all this was happening. Alfie wasn't usually so quiet and thoughtful. His mum realized that something wasn't quite right, but Alfie had to come up with a reason to put her off. He told her he was just tired, and after dinner he went upstairs to sit in his room and think. Settling into his favourite thinking spot, on the floor underneath his window with his back to the wall, Alfie finally had the peace and quiet he needed to take it all in.

In his hands he held a ball that had come from the National Space Centre. It was a globe, showing the continents of Earth and its big blue oceans. Usually when Alfie held it, it made him think how big the world was. Today it looked so small, now he knew the universe was full of so much else.

Alfie tossed it from hand to hand as he tried to make

sense of all Mr Monk had told him today.

Captain Venka had collected the two crates of cargo from two different planets. He was a sort of security guard or police officer, and he was trusted to take dangerous things to be stored where the wrong people couldn't find them.

It turned out that Captain Venka had been clever, hiding the ship in a parallel universe. There were so many universes, Mr Monk had explained, that you wouldn't stand a chance of finding it if you didn't know which one it was in.

Talking about the cargo, Alfie had laughed when Mr Monk had explained why a crate of frogs was considered so dangerous. Fajiro frogs were usually harmless, but if they ate something containing phenol, their intestinal gas became explosive when it met the air. The Fajiro frogs would fart fire, shooting flames six feet from their rear ends. The frogs were no danger on their home planet but they had been used as weapons on others where the gases in the atmosphere were different. Alfie wondered what was in the other crate – some other weird animal weapon?

The ship's computer had explained that to keep the vessel secure, the *Monkesto* had been locked to the DNA of the person operating it; Captain Venka. Only he could get on board and use the ship's systems. For some reason when Captain Venka's vital signs had been lost the key had reset.

Mr Monk didn't know why or how that could have happened. He said once the key was reset, it would have locked to whoever picked it up next. It was just chance that it had been Alfie, and not the Variado.

Alfie felt his stomach tighten like a fist every time he thought of the map, with those three lights on it. Captain Venka, Alfie and the Variado.

He must have run right past the thing. He hadn't seen anything, but he remembered that creepy feeling of being watched. The alien knew for sure that *someone* had picked up that key, and maybe it didn't know it was Alfie, or where Alfie lived, but it wouldn't give up so easily, would it? It must have shot down Captain Venka's ship for a reason.

Alfie really wanted to tell his parents. This whole thing was just too big for him to manage on his own. He was a kid! Spaceships stuck in other dimensions, weird alien cargo, disappearing life signs, shape-changing aliens! He was pretty sure this wasn't even adult stuff.

He kept making the choice to tell his mum and dad, almost standing up to go downstairs and then stopping. They wouldn't believe him.

He'd asked Mr Monk if he could bring them to the *Monkesto* to show them, but the computer had said no. The security settings on the ship meant only the operator was allowed onto the ship, no one else.

Even if Alfie did show his parents, was that the right thing to do? What about the planet Milito? Total destruction didn't sound like a great plan for Earth.

No matter how much he thought about it, Alfie just couldn't come up with a plan. All he knew was, while the key was locked to him, it was his problem to solve. His brain was fuzzy, his eyes were hot and itchy and he felt like a flat battery, with no energy to even think. He needed to sleep. Maybe he'd wake up in the morning with a plan.

Thirteen

Alfie stayed away from the *Monkesto* all day Sunday. His parents had made plans for the day and Alfie didn't think he could talk his way out of them. It had felt good to be outside, in the fresh air, doing things that were just fun. They'd hiked in the woods, built a den and played pooh sticks, and Alfie had been able to put thoughts of spaceships and aliens out of his head for a while. He felt lighter and his mind wasn't so busy and worried.

The routine of school on Monday morning was comforting too, even the way as soon as he got into the playground Omar jumped on him.

Alfie had known Omar since pre-school. They liked each other, but whenever they played together it would end up going wrong. Alfie had decided it was better to try and avoid Omar, but the bigger boy had a way of finding him.

'Get off!' Alfie complained as Omar clung to his back.

'Nope,' Omar replied. 'My legs hurt. I neeeeeed you to carry me around this morning.'

Alfie rolled his eyes, then tilted his shoulders down so Omar had no choice but to slide off.

'You suck!' Omar called as he ran away, laughing.

Just then, Amy appeared by Alfie's side. 'He's such a muppet,' she said. 'Where did you get to on Friday? I ran after you but couldn't find you anywhere.'

Alfie's cheeks felt hot and fizzy. He knew he had to mislead his friend and he didn't like it. 'I ran. We were uh, going out...' he trailed off. Not only did he hate lying, but he wasn't very good at it.

'Huh,' Amy didn't sound convinced, but she changed the subject. 'Did you hear? Mr Sloan is taking small groups today to do something special. Do you think we're going to launch a rocket? Remember that?'

Alfie remembered all right. He'd only been in reception at the time but the whole school had gone out to see the small rocket launch up into the sky and come back down on a parachute.

'That would be amazing!' Alfie said, forgetting all about his problems for a moment.

'Yeah,' Amy replied. 'Oh, there's Sally. I need to tell her something. Catch you later, Alfie.'

Alfie nodded, watching his best friend run off. Inside his pocket, his fingers ran over the sharp edges of the key. He hated not being able to share the *Monkesto* with Amy, even if he did understand why the secret had to be kept. He'd never kept anything big from her before. He'd never really kept secrets from anyone before. He needed to get good at it pretty quickly if he was going to hide from the Variado.

There was a real buzz amongst year six as they lined up for assembly. The rumour that Mr Sloan was going to do something special with them had spread quickly, and pretty much everyone had a different idea of what it might be. Would it be a rocket or some kind of science experiment? Someone suggested they might be making a movie using the tablet computers and editing it. There were lots of guesses but no facts.

The school hall was small, all the children had to squeeze up close together for assembly to get everyone in. The extra excitement from the older kids meant the hall was noisier than usual this morning, but everyone fell silent the moment Mr Sloan came in.

Rather than his usual smile and nod to the children, today Mr Sloan's face looked like it had been moulded from grumpy concrete. He didn't even say excuse me when he had to get past Miss Beavis. Even the way he walked today looked different, Alfie thought. He must have something serious to talk about.

'Sometimes, when you think you're doing the right thing, you can be doing the wrong one,' the head began, and Alfie realized he had been right. This wasn't going to be a fun assembly.

'Let's say, for example, that you find something that someone else has lost. What is the right thing to do?'

A few hands shot up from children ready to answer, but Mr Sloan ignored them.

'You might think that, if you don't know who it belongs to, that it is alright to keep it. There is an expression you have, "Finders keepers, losers weepers". Now, that doesn't sound very NICE, does it?'

Mr Sloan paused, taking time to look slowly around the hall. Any children who squirmed, coughed, or made any sort of reaction got a long, hard stare from the headmaster.

Alfie sat absolutely still, which was difficult because the more he thought about the key in his pocket, the bigger it felt. Alfie was sure other people must be able to see it, that any minute someone would point a finger at him and accuse him of stealing it.

He remembered his own strange reaction when he'd found the key, wanting to hide it, wanting to keep it. That was a side effect of the biological link, Mr Monk said, but it didn't make him feel any better about it now. He couldn't even tell the Skolto Service about the key, because the communication system on the *Monkesto* was broken. The key didn't just feel big; it felt heavy. The weight of the responsibility made Alfie feel sluggish and slow.

'You are just younglings. Children. You don't always know what is the right thing to do. You can't always tell if people are telling you the truth. Just because someone tells you that they are the good guys, can you believe them?'

Alfie blinked. An uncomfortable heaviness started in the middle of his stomach. The things that Mr Sloan was saying described what had been happening to Alfie so well. Did he really know that the Skolto Service were the good guys? He only had Mr Monk's word for it that they were the police, and the Variado was the bad guy.

'Until you are elders, and you understand the ways of the worlds…'

Alfie frowned. Had Mr Sloan just said worlds, plural? No, Alfie thought, he must have misheard. 'Until then, you should always ask an adult for help. If any of you have a problem, then you should tell someone. You should tell me.'

The headmaster didn't say another word. He just gave another one of those sweeping glances around the room, like a searchlight looking for the person who was acting the guiltiest. Then he stalked out of the hall and towards his office.

Alfie swallowed, getting up with the rest of his class to file out on wobbly legs. Was Mr Sloan right? Should he just take the key and give it to a grown up?

Fourteen

Alfie tried to concentrate and get on with his work, but whenever he moved the key dug into his leg and reminded him of the assembly that morning. Had he done the wrong thing, by picking up the key? If his family found things in the street, they put them where they could be seen, like on top of a gatepost. Why hadn't he done that?

Then there was the nasty suspicion that Mr Sloan had been right, that you shouldn't just do what people told you because you thought they were the good guys. Alfie had no way of knowing that what Mr Monk told him was the truth. Maybe the Skolto Service weren't the police, or the ship didn't really belong to them. Maybe the Variado *should* have the key. He only had Mr Monk's word for it that Variados were pirates.

Then he remembered the dots on the screen, and Captain Venka. The captain had been the operator of the *Monkesto* and something had happened to him. His vital signs had been lost. The only other beings in the alley at the time were Alfie and the Variado. It had to have been the Variado that did…whatever it had done. Someone had shot down the *Monkesto*, and someone had got rid of the captain. That sounded a lot like pirates!

Alfie pushed his lunch around on his plate, greasy gravy soaking into dry mash. That wasn't why Alfie had no appetite, though. It was because he couldn't shake one thought from his head: he shouldn't keep the key. Finding it was easily the most epic thing that had ever happened to him. He certainly didn't want to give up on the chance to go back to the *Monkesto*. He wanted to explore more, learn more about aliens and parallel dimensions...if he could persuade Mr Monk to tell him. A part of him knew that these weren't the sorts of problems that a kid was supposed to deal with by themselves. Should he ask for help?

He knew it was possible that the Variado had seen him pick up the key – maybe not well enough to know that it was him, Alfie Slider, who had the thing, but enough to start searching. If Alfie passed the key on, then even if the Variado found him, it wouldn't find the key. The ship would be safe.

Putting his knife and fork down, Alfie nodded to himself, certain that he was making the right choice.

'Why are you nodding?' Amy's question cut through his thoughts.

'Because he's one of those nodding dogs. Nod, nod, nod,' said Omar, nodding his head with his lips turned down in his best bulldog impression.

Alfie groaned. He'd been so deep in his own thoughts that he hadn't realized his friends had joined him at the table.

'Nothing.'

'You're nodding at nothing?' Amy said, raising her eyebrows and wrinkling up her nose like Alfie was some weird kind of bug she'd just spotted in her lunch.

'No. I mean...yes. Ugh!' Alfie frowned hard at both of them. 'I was just thinking about something, trying to decide what to do. I just realized what the right thing to do was.'

'Oh,' Amy said, piling food on her fork and popping it in her mouth.

'Is the right thing *fun?*' asked Omar.

'What?' Alfie thought Omar could be really random at times.

'I just think you should do the thing that's the most fun, that's all.'

'You don't know what you're talking about,' Alfie grumbled as he grabbed his plate and stood up. He could feel Amy watching him as he left, but he didn't look back. He took his plate up, scraped all the bits he hadn't eaten in his slop bucket and tidied his plate and cutlery away. After he wiped his hands, he walked quickly out of the hall, towards the headmaster's office.

When the door swung closed behind him it was wonderfully quiet, just for a moment. Alfie just stood there, feeling all the frustration of talking to Amy and Omar floating away like helium balloons. He didn't want to give up the key, give up the *Monkesto*. It was a hard decision and they hadn't helped, even if they had no idea what was going on. Reaching into his pocket, Alfie wrapped his fingers around the key and walked down the corridor towards Mr Sloan's office.

The door was standing open, and as he got close he could hear voices inside. It sounded like Mrs Noonan, who worked in the school office, and Mr Sloan. Alfie walked more hesitantly. He didn't want to eavesdrop, but he didn't want to disturb them if they were in the middle of something.

'You didn't recognize the child?' asked Mrs Noonan.

'No.'

'Boy or girl?'

'Short hair, trousers.'

'Probably a boy then but...maybe not,' Mrs Noonan replied. 'What year do you think they were in?'

'This year,' came Mr Sloan's reply.

There was a long pause, then Mrs Noonan coughed.

'Ummm. I mean school year? One of the older kids if they were walking home alone at that time? Year five or six?'

'That is logical.'

'You could maybe start with the children who were at clubs after school, but there were a few on that night. Football, tennis and, oh yes. Archery.'

Alfie shivered as an icy thought had popped into his head like brain freeze. It sounded a lot like Mr Sloan was looking for someone. It sounded a lot like Mr Sloan was looking for him!

'Here's a list of all the Year Five or Six children who were at clubs last night. If you can't find the child you want there, we can look again?'

'Yes.'

Alfie wasn't sure why, but he found himself spinning around and walking as fast as he could back up the corridor and into the hall. His hand was still tightly grasping at the key. He wasn't going to give it to Mr Sloan. With what Alfie had heard, Mr Sloan didn't feel like the sort of person he could trust at all.

Fifteen

Alfie sucked in a big breath of air as he went out into the playground, hoping it would cool his brain. He avoided making eye contact with anyone else, sitting down in a corner and hugging his knees. There were all sorts of thoughts going around in his head. Some of them had his own voice, but he could hear Mr Monk, his mum and Mr Sloan as well. Keep the key, said Alfie. Make a poster! said Mum. Protect the *Monkesto*, said Mr Monk. Tell your problems to a grown up, you're too young to know what to do! said his headmaster.

Alfie put his hands over his ears to try and quiet the thoughts, but you can't shut off the voices that come from inside. What was going on with Mr Sloan? What was the right thing to do? How had his life got so complicated?

Amy appeared in front of him, standing with her hands on her hips.

'What's up with you?' she asked.

'Nothing.'

Amy arched an eyebrow; she didn't believe him.

'Nothing!'

Amy tilted her head to one side and gave him "the

look". Normally when she did that, Alfie did whatever she wanted, but today he couldn't.

'Just leave me alone!' he exploded.

Dropping her hands to her side, Amy narrowed her eyes. Alfie waited for her to shout back, but she just turned and walked away. It was worse, somehow.

'Amy!' Alfie called after her, but she didn't turn back.

'Oh great! Perfect!' Alfie tucked himself further into the corner, closed his eyes and covered his ears. He stayed that way until the bell went and he had to get up and join the queue.

Amy was standing close to her friend Sally, their heads bent together as they talked quietly. Alfie tried to catch her eye, to apologize, but no matter where he moved Amy always had her back to him. Alfie thought that was probably on purpose. He'd upset her. He shouldn't have shouted.

As they were filing back into class Miss Beavis called out, 'Omar Syed, Alfie Slider, Miles Kennedy and Simon Shipton, you're all going to work with Mr Sloan this afternoon. Go into the hall. He has an activity set up for you.'

Alfie glanced towards Amy and saw she was looking right at him, her face said it all; first Alfie had upset her and now he'd been chosen to do something cool. Amy wasn't about to forgive him any time soon.

The boys all filed out, Omar in the front and Alfie bringing up the rear with his head down like a disgraced dog.

'Woah!' Omar gasped as he pushed ahead into the hall, blocking the entrance and the view. One of the other boys gave him a shove to get him through the doorway, then they all squeezed into the hall.

In the middle of the room were two, tall towers made up from pieces of gymnastics equipment stacked on top of each other. A wooden balance beam made a sort of bridge from one to the other. It was part of an obstacle course, Alfie thought. It must use just about every piece of PE kit the school had. Some of the course looked easy enough, just swinging on a rope from one bench to another, or running over some hurdles, but Alfie's eyes kept returning to those two tall towers.

His brain went into overdrive as he tried to work out what was going on. What were they supposed to do? Add to it, or did they have to make it safe? The worst option, the one that Alfie didn't really want to think about, was that they might be asked to *do* it.

Where was Mr Sloan, anyway? Alfie looked left, then right, almost jumping out of his skin when he saw the headmaster standing right next to him. How had he got there? Alfie hadn't seen or heard him walking up.

'Oh hello, sir,' Alfie said. 'What's this?' He pointed at the obstacle course.

Mr Sloan smiled, but it wasn't a nice smile. Usually when Mr Sloan did projects with the kids, you got an idea of what he must have been like as a child himself. He got excited. There was no childish sparkle in Mr Sloan's eyes today.

'You will complete the assault course, and I will time you. The quickest wins a prize!' The weird non-smile flashed again.

'For safety you must give me anything that you have

in your pockets.' He held out his hand, palm up, ready to take things from them.

Alfie hung back, letting the others hand over their stuff first. Mr Sloan just stared at whatever was put into his hand, even when Omar produced a used tissue. It looked like it was still damp, but Mr Sloan just inspected it and then put it onto a tray with the other things.

When it was Alfie's turn, he approached Mr Sloan and pulled a satsuma from his pocket. Putting it into the teacher's hands, he looked up to find Mr Sloan staring intently at the fruit. What was so fascinating about a satsuma?

Alfie jumped as the teacher's gaze snapped from the satsuma to him, the dark eyes locked onto Alfie's. Alfie felt a lump in his throat and he tried to swallow it down. It felt like Mr Sloan knew that he was hiding something.

'I'll go first!' Omar shouted, distracting Mr Sloan as he rushed to get ahead of the others and start the course. Alfie stood back; he was in no hurry to take his turn!

Omar was more enthusiastic about PE than he was able to do it. Miss Beavis always said he had a lot of determination, but whatever sport it was, Omar always looked awkward. Omar was showing determination now, as he pushed his way along the floor underneath some netting.

Emerging at the other side, he had to run around some cones in a slalom and then climb the rope ladder. The ladder led up to the top of the first tower. It was only when Omar was about halfway up, out of breath and starting to look scared, that Alfie realized there were no mats on the ground at either side. What if someone fell…?

Alfie turned to Mr Sloan and said, 'Umm, sir. Is that safe?'

The teacher didn't answer. Alfie realized Mr Sloan was standing staring at Omar with a strange, almost hungry, look in his eyes. Why didn't he have a stopwatch? Wasn't he supposed to be timing them?

Even from this distance, Alfie could see that Omar was afraid. Omar was crawling along the course instead of walking, and every now and then made a little whimpering noise like a sad puppy. Almost like he was answering, Mr Sloan made a quiet, hissing noise.

'I can't watch!' someone said.

Alfie had the opposite problem; he couldn't *not* watch. Omar was a chunky boy, and the beam was narrow. Holding his breath, Alfie crossed his fingers, hoping Omar would make it across with no problem.

When Omar was halfway, Alfie almost relaxed. Then Omar squealed as his whole body tipped to one side. Everything went into slow motion. Alfie watched, helpless, as the boy toppled off the beam and fell to the floor with a horrid crunch.

Alfie ran towards Omar. As he passed Mr Sloan, the headmaster said something. Alfie's brain wouldn't quite process the words. It had sounded a lot like "puny humans".

Kneeling down by Omar, Alfie wanted to give the boy all his attention but there was a little voice in his head that was telling him that he was in way more trouble than Omar. That wasn't Mr Sloan. That was the Variado!

Sixteen

Omar was lying on his side, crying. He was holding onto one of his arms with the other hand. Alfie ran up, unsure what to do. He tried to remember what you did in an accident, and remembered how you should calm the person down, let them know it's going to be OK.

'It's alright, Omar. We'll get some help,' Alfie said. He put his hand on the other boy's shoulder, then pulled it back, worried he was hurting him.

Alfie looked up to see the headmaster walking calmly out of the hall. Not towards the office to get help, but into the corridor outside their classroom.

The other boys were still frozen in place where they had been, their faces pinched and worried. This was the time when a grown-up usually told you what to do, and they were still waiting for that.

'Go get help!' Alfie shouted. It was like he'd woken the boys up. They widened their eyes, nodded and ran together towards the door that led to the office.

Alfie carried on talking to Omar, trying to be calming and encouraging. Omar wasn't crying so hard now, but he was still sniffling and whimpering. Alfie felt his eyes filling up with sympathy, but he didn't have time to be distracted. Was his headmaster an alien?

A loud noise from the other side of the hall made him look up. Mr Sloan was in the corridor outside, opening locker doors and then slamming them shut again. Alfie felt like worms were squirming around in his belly. Had the alien set this whole thing up so it could search for the key? Was that why it had wanted them to empty their pockets, was that why Omar had been made to do that ridiculous obstacle course?

The next few minutes were a blur of activity. People came to help, getting Alfie and the others to sit down in the quiet of the school office and have a drink of water and a biscuit. Someone who knew first aid stayed with Omar until the ambulance came. Alfie was really relieved to see that Omar walked out to it himself, his arm tied up in a temporary sling.

Alfie couldn't stop shaking, like he was strapped to a pneumatic drill. Shock, they told him, but he knew it was more than just that. It was fear.

The only way he could explain what had happened was that the Variado had taken the headmaster's place. But where was Mr Sloan, the real Mr Sloan, now? He knew the Variado was looking for the key. Thoughts were running through Alfie's mind at top speed as he tried to come up with a plan to throw the alien off the scent.

Mrs Noonan had to tell him three times before he realized he was being allowed to go home early. His brain felt all slow and mushy. School had rung their parents, who were on their way. The other boys were collected, Simon by his gran and Miles by his dad, and not long after came Mum with Lizzie in tow.

'Oh, love! You're white as a sheet!' Mum said when she arrived. She swooped in to give Alfie the inevitable hug and kiss. 'What a nasty shock.'

Alfie nodded, blinking back tears.

'Let's get you home.'

Mum put a gentle hand on his back and pushed him towards the door. She stopped by the reception desk and handed a piece of paper to Mrs Noonan. 'Sorry, but could you put that up on the notice board for me? When things have calmed down.'

Alfie focused on the paper. It said 'Have you lost a key? Found near Stitcher Street. No key ring.' It gave their family name and phone number.

'Mum, no!' Alfie groaned in protest.

'Oh, I know, love. Sorry. Let's go.'

What could Alfie do? His mum had no idea why what she was doing was such a bad thing. He could hardly tell her. He tried to turn and grab the poster, but Mum's hand was firm at his back. Alfie felt sicker when he saw a tall figure walk into the office and stand beside Mrs Noonan. Staring at the poster with the first real smile that Alfie had seen on his face since this whole thing began was Mr Sloan. No, the Variado.

Ducking his head to hide his expression, Alfie let his mum walk him out the door and home. His heart and mind were racing. Thanks to his mum, the Variado knew he had the key! What could he do now?

Seventeen

Alfie woke to the disorienting feeling that it was later than it should be. A panicked glance at his alarm clock showed him it was gone nine. He should be in school! He was halfway out of bed before his sluggish brain reminded him that he didn't need to go today.

Last night, his parents had been worried about him. He was pale, they said, and distracted. They were worried that the shock of seeing Omar fall had affected Alfie, and decided that he needed a day at home to recover. Alfie wasn't about to disagree. The last thing he wanted to do was go into school. The Variado could get to him easily there; one false move and he'd be sent to the headmaster's office. Sent straight to the alien wearing his headmaster's face.

There was one disadvantage to being home sick. Alfie really needed to get to the *Monkesto* to talk to Mr Monk. Usually, if he was off sick his mum wanted him to rest. She sometimes even said no TV. She always wanted him to be calm and quiet. How could he convince her to let him go out by himself today?

Alfie got dressed and then went downstairs trying to

think of something to say, or do, to get what he needed. How do you walk when you're too shocked to go to school, but well enough to go out, he wondered? Alfie tried to balance looking worried with being fidgety. He started by choosing a book from the shelf, but just leafing through it idly and sighing a lot, then putting it back. Next, he got out his toy soldiers, and started lining them up but then just scooped them up and put them back in the box.

It must have worked because mid-morning his mum said, 'I'm taking Lizzie to the park. Do you want to come along?'

Alfie shook his head. 'No.' A thought nudged its way onto his tongue, 'I think I'd be worried, seeing Lizzie on the climbing frame.'

He dared a glance at Mum and saw her face crumple up with concern. Alfie quickly looked away before he lost his nerve, 'But can I go for a walk? I think I just need some time by myself.' He held his breath as he waited to see if she'd go for it.

'Alright.' Mum said, after thinking for a few seconds. 'Maybe being outdoors in the fresh air is just what you need.'

Alfie nodded while his stomach swirled with a mixture of relief and guilt. His parents had always told him the one thing they really hated was lying, and now he couldn't seem to do anything else, but what else could he do?

They left the house together, but when they got to the end of the drive Mum and Lizzie went one way towards the park, and Alfie went the other towards the alley. As soon as they were out of sight, Alfie started running.

A thought hit the brakes as he got to the entrance to the alley. Alfie came to a dead stop. It wasn't that long ago that he'd found Mr Sloan lurking in the alley, would he be there again now?

Alfie walked slowly, checking up and down the alley, making sure he was alone. When he was certain there was no one around, he braced himself to transport to the *Monkesto*, a flicker of excitement tickling his belly. Teleporting to your own spaceship wasn't going to get boring any time soon.

It was only when he got on board and his shoulders relaxed that he realized how tense he'd been. He was safe here, though. No one but him could get on board.

The system whirred into life as always. Today Alfie didn't bother with a greeting he was sure the computer would ignore, he just started straight in with a question.

'Where is Mr Sloan?'

There was no answer for a minute, then Mr Monk said, 'Locating...'

A map of the world appeared on the screen, and narrowed down first to Europe, then England, zooming closer and closer until it was centred on a farmer's field just outside Alfie's village. Alfie waited for an explanation but it didn't come.

'Is he alright?'

'Vital signs are stable,' Mr Monk spoke finally. 'Vital signs are consistent with Mr Sloan being in suspended animation.'

'Yes!' Alfie punched the air in relief. He had been worried that Mr Sloan was hurt, or worse. He knew suspended animation was probably alright. At least, it had been OK for his sea monkeys – their eggs lasted in suspended animation for ages.

'Sensors indicate that Mr Sloan is on board a spacefaring vessel,' Mr Monk replied.

'The Variado switched places,' Alfie said, nodding. 'It's at my school. It looks like the head teacher. It's looking for the key.'

'Alfie Slider, as operator of the *Monkesto* you are the only one who can prevent this vessel and its cargo from falling into the wrong hands,' Mr Monk said.

'Yes, I get that.' Alfie grumbled. 'The thing is I'm a kid. What am I supposed to do about it?'

'You have the *Monkesto* at your disposal,' Mr Monk answered.

Alfie supposed he was trying to be reassuring. 'Great, a spaceship stuck in a parallel universe. Loads of help. Great for *me* to hide in but useless when that thing turns up at my house asking for the key!'

When there was no reply, Alfie asked, 'Will Mr Sloan be alright if I can get the Variado to let him go?'

'There are no long-lasting side effects from suspended animation.'

'Alright. Then I just have to work out how to get the Variado to give him back,' Alfie decided, getting up from his seat and walking back towards the red dot of the transport hub.

'Alfie Slider, you must not let the Variado gain access to this vessel,' Mr Monk replied.

'Return,' Alfie said firmly. He wasn't promising anything. It seemed to him that the easiest way to solve this whole mess was to just give the shape-changer what it wanted so it would leave him alone. No one else would get hurt, and Alfie wouldn't have to worry that the alien was waiting for him around every corner.

'Alfie Slider, you must not let the Variado gain access to this vessel.' The computer spoke again, in exactly the same tone of voice.

'What do you expect me to DO?' Alfie shouted.

'Alfie Slider, you must not let the Variado gain access to this vessel.'

Alfie stood still, hands balled into a fist at his side. Anger was whirling around inside his body, he felt like he was made from molten metal. He was angry with Mr Monk, with the Variado and with himself for having picked up the stupid key in the first place.

'Alright!' he shouted, 'Alright. I'll find a way.'

The moment he had spoken, Mr Monk started the transport and he was returned back to the alley.

Eighteen

Alfie sat cross-legged on the floor, surrounded by bits of wire and electronics. He'd thought that if he spent some time trying to build the model spaceship he'd got for his birthday, it might take his mind off things. So far, it wasn't working. He'd get so far, and then just drift off and start worrying about what he was going to do all over again.

The Variado knew he had the key. What did the Variado want, though? They key itself, so it could get to the *Monkesto*? Or just the cargo? Those crazy fire-farting frogs, perhaps? Well, maybe not those. Alfie let out a big sigh, blinked back into reality and saw his sister had appeared right in front of him.

Lizzie was holding her hand out like she expected Alfie to give her something. Her head was tilted to one side and she was doing what he called her crazy eyes. He realized that she must have asked him for something, and he'd been too spaced out to hear her.

'Sorry, Liz, what?' he asked.

'Can I build your spaceship?' Lizzie asked, adding after a moment's thought, 'Please?'

Alfie immediately started shaking his head, 'Sorry, Liz, no. The parts are delicate and you might break them.'

'I wouldn't!'

'I know you wouldn't mean to, but you might by accident,' Alfie said.

Lizzie wasn't impressed with that answer. The crazy eyes only got crazier, and her hands went to her hips. Lizzie looked liked a mini version of his mum, getting ready to tell him off. Alfie looked down at all the parts that were in front of him, wondering what he could do to stop Lizzie getting more upset. A thought started tickling inside his brain. 'Hey, do you know what, Lizzie? There is something you could help me with.'

Lizzie had just opened her mouth. Alfie thought she was probably getting ready to tell Mum how mean he was being, that he wasn't sharing. When he spoke she snapped her jaw shut again and settled for a pout instead.

'What?' she asked.

Alfie knew this was a delicate part of the negotiation. He had to make it seem real to Lizzie, like she was really helping and that he was giving her a real job, not a baby job.

'There are these pieces here that need to be clicked together. I'm worried if I do them that I might break them. Could you do it for me? You're always so careful.'

Lizzie stared at him, lips pursed and eyes narrowed. Alfie could see her thinking it all over. Moments later her face relaxed and she plopped down on the floor beside him with a big smile and picked up the parts he pushed towards her.

That thought in his brain started tickling again.

What if, he thought, he could do the same thing with the Variado? What if, he could persuade it that it couldn't have the *Monkesto* but it could have the cargo? It probably didn't know what was on board, so what if Alfie convinced it that the cargo was valuable or mysterious?

Alfie still wasn't sure if it was a very good plan, but it was a lot better than no plan which was all he'd had before. He smiled at his sister, leaned over and gave her a kiss.

'I love you, Lizzie,' he said.

Lizzie smiled, snuggled against him for a second and then got on with clicking the pieces together. Alfie watched Lizzie with an indulgent smile. In that moment things didn't seem so impossible after all. At least, they weren't as long as shape-shifting pirate aliens could compromise as well as a four-year-old.

Nineteen

Alfie had set his alarm to wake him early the next morning. He'd told Mum he wanted to go to a friend's house on the way to school, to work on his story again. It didn't feel like such a big lie, this time. That was partly because he had started thinking of Mr Monk as a friend, but also because now he had the beginnings of a plan he was hoping the need for secrets would soon be over.

He'd taken a couple of slices of toast and a carton of juice with him so he could eat breakfast while he talked his idea over with Mr Monk. First though, he had to see if it would work at all.

There was no one else about as Alfie walked to the alley. No one walking their dogs or out for an early morning run. Alfie had the streets to himself and was quickly back on board the *Monkesto*, listening to the whirr as the systems warmed up.

'Mr Monk, will you open the door to the cargo bay?' he asked, turning around on the red dot of the transport hub to face the door to the rear.

The door opened and Alfie stepped through, expecting to go into a room the same size as the bridge. What he actually stepped into was more like a cupboard, a small, square room that had a door directly opposite with a panel beside it covered in lights and switches.

Alfie opened his mouth to complain to the computer, when the door behind him closed and right away the one opposite opened. There was the cargo bay he had been expecting!

The other half of the dome was mostly empty space. The room was exactly the same shape as the control room, but with no console or chair. No screen. All that was in the room were two, very shiny, silver crates. Alfie walked slowly around them, checking if there was anything on the outside that showed what was inside.

There wasn't. Not a label, not a marking, not a picture. Nothing. Alfie felt his confidence grow. He walked all the way around them again, double-checking, then said, 'Mr Monk, I want to go back to the control room.'

The door in front opened, letting him into that small square room, and then through to the control room. Alfie wondered if that strange, in between space was an airlock. Maybe it was for safety or decontamination. So nothing nasty could get from the cargo bay to the flight deck.

'Mr Monk, I have an idea,' Alfie began. 'Can I take things off the *Monkesto*?'

'You can. You may either take things in your arms, or use the ship's transport beam.'

Alfie grinned. He had hoped that the transport system didn't just work on people, but that he could use it to transport things as well.

'I'm going to make a deal with the Variado, get him to give me back the real Mr Sloan—' Alfie began.

'Alfie Slider, you must not let the Variado gain access to this vessel.'

It was exactly the same words as Mr Monk had used yesterday. It made Alfie's skin crawl. He kept forgetting Mr Monk wasn't a person, and it made him uneasy to be reminded he was talking to a computer.

'I know,' Alfie replied, impatiently, 'I'm not going to. I'm going to give him the crate of Fajiro frogs.'

There was no reply from Mr Monk.

'There's no way he can know what's in the crate, right?'

Mr Monk replied, 'Correct. The flight plan and manifesto of the *Monkesto* were top secret. The most likely scenario is that it was chance that the two ships encountered each other in this part of space. The crates are resistant to scans, so it will be unable to determine the contents without opening it.'

Alfie nodded, the first genuine smile wriggling onto his lips for days.

'So, tell me a bit about Variados so I can work out how to convince it this is the best way?'

The screen pinged into life, showing the same basic information about the Variado as it had before.

'The Variado are an opportunistic race. They claim to make their money through salvaging unwanted and irreparable vessels and breaking them down for parts,' Mr Monk began.

'Like the scrap man?' Alfie mused.

'Indeed. However, they have a reputation for boarding vessels and taking them by force, stealing the cargo. Piracy.'

Alfie chewed on one side of his lip, wondering how

he could persuade a pirate to ignore a ship and just take a crate instead.

'There are also unsubstantiated rumours about Variados altering safety beacons and allowing vessels to run into trouble,' continued Mr Monk.

'Wreckers?' Alfie said.

'Indeed,' came the swift reply.

A helpful memory popped into Alfie's head. They'd been on holiday to Cornwall once and heard stories about wreckers. They would turn out the lighthouse and let a ship run aground on rocks, then go and steal the cargo. They didn't care if people died; they just took what they wanted. Alfie felt his belly twist in fear. How was he supposed to negotiate with an alien who thought like that? Then that familiar fizzing sensation of an idea he couldn't explain yet started in his brain. What were smugglers and wreckers afraid of? The Customs men!

'They wouldn't want the Skolto Service to find them, then?'

'That is correct,' answered the computer.

'So...' The words came slowly at first as Alfie thought his idea through. 'If I tell it that the *Monkesto* is stuck in another dimension, and needs lots of repairs. Make it seem like it's not worth the trouble. And I tell it that the Skolto Service are on their way, due any minute. Then I say, "but if you leave me alone then you can have this crate and whatever is in it?" Do you think that would work?'

The ship's computer didn't reply for a moment, then the familiar voice said, 'It is possible, but that is a dangerous plan, Alfie Slider.'

'Oh really? Now you say it's dangerous? Thanks a flipping lot!' Alfie felt the heat of anger rising in him again, out of nowhere. 'It's not like I hadn't realized that already. I can't do nothing, though. Mr Sloan is in suspended animation, the Variado has already hurt one of my friends and it knows where I live! Doing nothing is dangerous too!'

'Agreed,' replied Mr Monk. 'There is just one thing you may not be taking into consideration. Something reset the key, so it was no longer locked to Captain Venka. His vital signs were lost. It is logical to assume that the Variado made that happen. We don't know how, there is no record in my data banks of technology that could do that. This could happen to you too, Alfie Slider. I can suggest no defence against unknown technology.'

Alfie sighed, slumping down into the seat by the control panel. 'You're right,' he said, feeling the excitement go out of him like the air from a punctured balloon.

'However,' Mr Monk continued, 'if the Variado could do this easily, it would have done it by now. It seems logical that the Variado would want you to be alone, to avoid the wrong person picking up the key.'

Alfie nodded, that made sense. The Variado wouldn't want to risk another kid charging in and picking up the key.

'You should avoid being alone with the Variado, Alfie Slider.'

Alfie let out another sigh. 'Alright. So, I need to find the Variado and make a deal with it but I have to do that without being alone with it. I've got to spend the day at school without anyone sending me to the headmaster, even if he asks them to. I'm the only one who knows that it's an alien! No problem then, that sounds nice and easy.'

As if it wanted to add to the pressure, Alfie's watch chose that moment to beep. If he didn't get a move on he was going to be late for school.

'Alright, Mr Monk. Hopefully I'll make it through the day and I'll be back later.'

The computer didn't reply, and Alfie shook his head in disbelief. Just a few weeks ago he was worried about getting sent to the headmaster's office to be told off. The old Mr Sloan didn't seem anywhere near so scary now!

Twenty

Alfie skidded into the school playground just before the bell rang. Like any other day, kids were stood in groups talking or running backwards and forwards. The air was filled with a host of noises from excited whispers right up to screams of playful fear.

Alfie had just spotted Amy, deep in conversation with Sally, when the bell rang and they had to line up in front of their teachers. It was only then that Alfie noticed that the staff all looked serious. Alfie scanned their faces but couldn't see a single smile, just furrowed brows and downturned lips.

The teachers continued to act oddly, murmuring to each other and looking worried but otherwise the school day went on its usual routine. Alfie was a bag of nerves, jumping at the slightest thing and feeling a hard knot in his stomach just waiting for the Variado, wearing Mr Sloan's face to appear around a corner.

One word from the Variado, and Alfie would *have* to go with it. There was no excuse he could think of to avoid it. Everyone else thought it was the headmaster. How was he supposed to concentrate with worries like that swirling around in his mind?

Alfie kept finding himself just staring at the classroom door, waiting for the Variado to step in. He knew he was frustrating Miss Beavis; she'd just called his name and her tone let him know that it was at least the second time she'd done it. Earlier in the week he'd almost got sent to Mr Sloan for that, so he couldn't make that mistake again. He'd deliver himself right into the lion's den.

Time passed so slowly, like every moment was being stretched out like Silly Putty. As if all that wasn't bad enough, Amy was after him too!

She'd grabbed his arm at break time and asked him flat out, 'What's up with you?'

He'd mumbled something about having a headache but her nose wrinkled up in what Alfie thought of as her unimpressed face. Amy was smart, and they'd known each other for ages. He had a horrible feeling that she knew he wasn't being honest with her.

When lunchtime arrived and there was still no sign of the Variado, Alfie couldn't take it any more. Instead of standing in line for his school dinner, he slipped out of the hall and into the corridor near the office. He filled his lungs with air and let it out slowly, trying to find his calm and his courage.

Alfie had planned ahead, putting a piece of paper and a pen into his pocket so he could leave a note for the Variado if it wasn't in the office. He couldn't believe his luck to have got through so much of the day without seeing the alien.

Alfie sat down on the chairs outside the school office and applied himself to the problem. How do you write a coded message to an alien, arranging to swap your headmaster for some cargo? Alfie found himself just staring dumbly at the blank paper, pen in hand but clueless.

It took a while before he realized that he could hear voices, coming from the office, speaking really quietly like they didn't want to be overheard. He knew that he shouldn't really be listening, but when one of them said, 'Mr Sloan,' his ears tuned straight in.

'So where did they find him?' asked one voice.

'Edge of the village, just wandering on the road,' said another, and Alfie thought that sounded like Mrs Noonan.

'What was he doing out there?' asked the first voice.

'No idea. He doesn't remember either. He can't remember most of the last week, apparently. Doesn't remember what happened with Omar Syed, none of it. They've taken him into hospital – seems like some kind of breakdown.'

'Oh dear,' the other lady replied, 'There were no signs, were there? He seemed fine the last time I saw him.'

'Nothing at all. He was right as ninepence,' Mrs Noonan agreed.

Alfie hardly dared breathe. He was pretty sure that he shouldn't have heard any of that, but really, really glad that he had.

There was only one explanation that he could think of: the Variado had let Mr Sloan go. It must have realized that it had drawn too much attention to itself when Omar got hurt.

Besides, it had learnt what it needed to know; Alfie had the key. If Alfie had no clue what face it was wearing now, it would be much easier for the Variado to get close enough to try and steal the key.

A wave of dizziness crashed over Alfie as the situation became clear to him. The Variado could be anyone. *Anyone.* It wasn't safe for him to be alone with anyone at all!

Twenty-One

Perched right at the top of the climbing frame, at the highest point in the playground, Alfie sat and watched. From here he could see all of the school site, so no one would be able to creep up on him. His mind was working at one hundred miles an hour. If the Variado wasn't Mr Sloan any more, then who was it? Who would it try to be next, to get him alone?

Chewing his lip anxiously, Alfie scanned the faces of the staff but none of them were acting like an alien. Would it risk trying the same trick twice anyway? It would look suspicious if two teachers had breakdowns in one week.

As he watched a boy running after a football, Alfie noticed there was a man stood just outside the school fence. He wasn't moving. He was just staring straight ahead of him. Straight at Alfie.

Alfie's stomach clenched as he leaned forward, watching every move the man made. Could it be? That was weird, right? To just stand outside the fence and stare in?

Alfie felt more and more sure that this was the Variado. He was just standing up to walk to the fence and confront it when a little dog ran into view. The man seemed to snap out of his vacant, staring state and bent down to pick up the small dog's mess.

I don't think Variados would clean up dog poo, Alfie thought. He swallowed, trying to calm himself down again.

Because he'd been focusing so intently on the man, Alfie had taken his attention off the playground. He almost jumped out of his skin when Amy's head popped up over the top of the ladder.

'Hey, Amy,' he greeted, sitting back down. Amy didn't reply.

Odd, Alfie thought. She wasn't usually short of things to say.

Alfie watched his friend curiously as she pulled herself up from the ladder onto the platform and walked towards him. She still didn't say anything, just stopped in front of him and stood with her arms crossed, glaring coldly. The silence dragged on.

Alfie felt the colour draining out of his face and landing heavily in the pit of his stomach. Of course! Who better for the Variado to take over but his best friend? Who else would Alfie trust enough to be alone with, now, knowing the alien had moved on from Mr Sloan?

Standing up, Alfie forced his arms down by his side. He didn't want to give the Variado any clue that he had the key with him, still tucked into his pocket.

'You can have whatever you want.' Alfie said, doing his best to keep the wobble out of his voice. 'I'll swap you. For Amy. You better not have hurt her!' The anger came on so fast that Alfie felt the pressure of tears behind his eyes. He swallowed hard, the last thing he wanted to do was cry in front of the alien, but the thought of anything happening to his best friend was almost more than he could stand.

'What *are* you talking about, Alfie?' The voice was so completely Amy that all Alfie's worries disappeared in a moment. 'What are you going to swap? Who do you think I've hurt?'

'Oh, er, nothing, Amy.'

Alfie just stood there, grinning like an idiot. Even if Amy was telling him off, it was Amy. She hadn't been captured by a Variado, and every part of Alfie's body felt like it was dancing in celebration.

'What's up with you lately? You're being weird. Weird*er*.' Amy looked more than just unimpressed now. Alfie had never seen her so angry. She was clenching her fists so tightly Alfie was worried she was going to hurt herself, or punch him.

A wave of guilt hit him in the guts. He'd been so tied up in the *Monkesto* and everything that he hadn't been paying attention to his best friend.

'I'm sorry, Ames. I've had a lot going on. I'm just…' He let out a breath. 'It's hard to explain.'

'Try.'

Amy might not be the Variado but she was certainly giving Alfie a hard time.

'I can't. I just can't. I'm sorry.' Alfie did his best to sound as really and truly sorry as he was.

Amy just stared him down. 'Alright. If you don't want to be best friends any more then that's fine. See if I care, Alfie Slider!'

Before Alfie could say anything, Amy had spun on the

spot, made the jump to the fireman's pole and was sliding down.

'Amy! No! It's not like that!' Alfie called, but she didn't even slow down. Growling in frustration, he made a fist and punched the side of the climbing frame. The pain shocked him out of his anger, giving him something small that he could focus on.

Sighing, and rubbing his sore hand, Alfie couldn't believe that things were getting worse. If it wasn't enough that he had a shape-shifting alien after him, now he was losing his best friend too!

Twenty-Two

Somehow, Alfie thought, the afternoon was dragging worse than the morning. If it wasn't Miss Beavis getting frustrated that Alfie couldn't concentrate, it was Amy's hard stares from across the room. Alfie just felt like everything was spiralling out of his control.

He really wanted to tell Amy. Not just because she was his best friend, but also because she was the one that thought up all the good ideas. He could really use some good ideas just now.

The bell rang to bring an end to the school day, and Alfie let out a loud huff of air in relief. He hung back; he didn't want to run into Amy until he had some idea of what to say to her. Maybe he would have a better idea tomorrow, after he'd slept on it.

When the bustle of the corridor had calmed to just a few locker doors shutting, Alfie left the classroom. He wasn't going home just yet anyway; he was practising with his dance group for an hour.

Peeking through the door into the hall, he could see Mrs Green, his dance teacher, getting ready. She was smiling her usual smile as she talked to some of the other kids in the group. It was odd, Alfie thought, how he could be relieved that the Variado hadn't become Mrs Green, but also disappointed at the same time.

Alfie just wanted this to be over, right now. It was so frustrating! He had a plan, and could get the Variado off his back, but he couldn't find the alien to tell it that. It should all be over now. No more horrible feelings of being watched, of not knowing who he could trust. The tension was really getting to Alfie. He was tired, irritable and lonely.

As soon as dance was finished, Alfie gathered up his stuff and ran out of school. He was almost at the gate when he realized that he was the last one to leave. There was no crowd of other kids for him to get lost in, if the Variado was watching, there was nowhere for Alfie to hide.

The alien had been disguised as his headmaster for days, so it would know his timetable. He'd been looking over his shoulder all day, but he should have been thinking ahead. He should have been thinking about an ambush.

The Variado would be in the alley, waiting for him. As soon as he had the idea, Alfie was absolutely sure of it. He was also absolutely sure that he didn't want to meet the Variado there. That was where it had done…whatever it had done to Captain Venka. Alfie was definitely against anyone messing with his vital signs.

Rather than go home the normal route, Alfie decided it was safer to walk the long way. It would also give him some thinking time. At the moment he didn't even have a bad idea for what to do, but it felt good to at least be trying to do something. The long way took him along the busier roads, past the corner shop, and past Amy's house.

He hadn't even planned to do it, but when he got to her street he found his feet walking up her drive. His brain was saying "Don't get her involved" but his hand came up and knocked on the door anyway.

Alfie felt like he was a passenger inside his own head. He could only watch as the door opened to show his friends face, her brows arching in a challenge as she saw him.

'Yes?' Amy crossed her arms and her nose tilted in the air like Alfie was a bad smell.

Alfie felt all the words he'd been holding in just burst through his common sense.

'Amy, I'm really sorry. You're right. I've been a rubbish friend. There's something HUGE going on for me right now and I've been scared to tell you because I can't prove it. I need you to know, though. Will you hear me out?' Alfie only dared to look at Amy's eyes when he'd finished, hoping his very best puppy dog look would seal the deal.

'Alright. Come in,' Amy said, leading Alfie in and through the house, past her mum, to the back garden. They'd sat here side by side so many times over the years. It was comforting for Alfie. Memories of all the other times they'd sat like this, and Amy had helped him, made him feel a bit less hopeless.

'Just listen, OK? I know this is going to sound crazy, but please just listen?' Alfie asked, and when Amy agreed with a nod, he started to tell her the whole story.

He didn't look at her. He was too worried what her reaction would be. It was only when he had brought her right up to date, with Mr Sloan's breakdown, that he dared look across.

Amy's face was blank, no expression. She just sat there

looking at him, blinking. Alfie had no idea what she was thinking.

'If you're telling me the truth then you're the world's biggest idiot,' Amy said, finally.

Alfie's jaw dropped open in surprise. A few seconds later he managed to stutter, 'I am?'

'You can find out where the Variado is *easily*. Just go to the ship and use the scanners.'

She didn't actually say "duh!" but she might as well have done.

'Amy, you're amazing!' Alfie couldn't help it, the impulse to hug his friend was too much to resist. Just moments later though, reality sank in as he said, 'The only trouble is, the only access point that I know about is in the alleyway, and the Variado might be there. I can't be alone with it.'

Then the most brilliant thing ever happened.

Amy said, 'You don't have to be.'

Twenty-Three

'The Variado will expect me to come from school, so we'll go into the alley from the other direction,' Alfie decided, as they walked towards the street the alley opened on to.

Amy gave a quick, nervous nod of agreement. 'I'll go first,' she said, the words tripping out quickly. 'It's not looking for me, so I'll be fine.'

'No!' Alfie blurted, the thought of Amy being near the Variado had made him feel instantly dizzy, his stomach lurching.

'I'm not asking you, Alfie. I'm telling you.'

Before Alfie had a chance to say anything else she started running. Amy was quicker than him. He could always overtake her over long distances but in sprints, Amy had him every time. Knowing it was hopeless to try and catch up, Alfie ran as fast as he could after his friend. He didn't want her running into danger alone.

Sprinting into the street by the alley entrance, Alfie saw Amy had slowed to a walk. He kept running until he was beside her.

'Don't do that again!' he hissed. 'This is dangerous, Amy. I mean it.'

Amy just rolled her eyes at him and pointed up the alley, 'Can't see anyone.'

They walked slowly together until they got to the corner, when Amy pushed Alfie back and peeked around it herself.

'Nothing,' she whispered a moment later, then more loudly, 'There's no one here.'

Alfie peeped around himself, just to check, then sighed, 'Well, where is it then? An ambush made sense...' He shrugged. 'I'll have to go to the *Monkesto* and find out where it is, but I can't take you. The security, you know? Will you wait here?'

Amy nodded, but there was something strange about her expression now. She didn't look excited, or scared, she just looked...worried.

'What?' Alfie asked.

'Nothing.' Amy pressed her lips together tightly.

'Uh uh! You don't get to do that to me. You yelled at me earlier for keeping things from you!'

'I don't know, Alfie. It's just...if there had been someone here then it would have been proof. But there isn't, and...' Amy trailed off, then added miserably, 'What if you're sick?'

'In the head, you mean?' Alfie replied angrily, 'Just because the Variado isn't here doesn't mean it doesn't exist!'

'Alright. Calm down,' Amy said, like his mum did when Lizzie was about to have a tantrum.

'Calm down? You just called me crazy!'

It wasn't fair, Alfie thought. He was doing his best in a really tough situation, and he was being called crazy for it!

'Let's just go home,' Amy said.

'No,' Alfie said, feeling the anger roaring inside him like a gale force wind. He'd been so happy when he thought she'd just believed him. He'd thought she was the best friend in the world but now it turned out she was testing him. Well, he might not be able to take her to the *Monkesto* but there was something he could show her!

'I'm not going home. I'm going to *my* spaceship,' he shouted, pulling the key from his pocket and running towards the keyhole.

'Alfie!' Amy shouted.

It was the last sound Alfie heard before that whooshing, rushing feeling overtook him and he was transported to the deck of the *Monkesto*.

Twenty-four

Alfie was grinning with triumph as he found himself stood back in the control room of the *Monkesto* again. Take that, Amy! Crazy, was he? He would give anything to see her face right now. Wait, maybe he could!

'Mr Monk, do your scanners work like cameras? Can I see the alley?'

Alfie knew he'd have to wait for an answer until the system had finished initializing, and tapped his fingers impatiently on the control panel as he waited.

'Not without modification, Alfie Slider.'

'Shame,' Alfie said, running a hand through his hair as he got down to business. As much fun as it would be to see Amy's face right now, there were more important things to deal with.

'Mr Monk, where is Mr Sloan?'

As usual when he asked that kind of question the screen showed the whole of the earth, then quickly zoomed down to Europe, then England. Unlike last time when the dot had been in a field near the village, this time it was in a built up area of the nearby town. Alfie thought the location looked about right for the hospital.

'Is he alright?'

'Mr Sloan is outside the range of this vessel's vital sign scanners,' Mr Monk replied. 'He is at the hospital. Accessing his medical file…'

Alfie blinked. Mr Monk was doing what?

'Wait, no! That's private!' Alfie shouted, just as the computer spoke again.

'Mr Sloan is physically well.'

Alfie puffed his cheeks out, and let the breath out slowly, 'Good.'

It was great news that his headmaster was all right, that he was at the hospital. It was scary how easily Mr Monk had got into the medical files. How had he done that? What else could the computer find out? Focus, Alfie whispered to himself.

'Alright. The Variado was getting too much attention as Mr Sloan. I think it let him go – the poor guy thinks he had a breakdown or something,' Alfie said.

'That would be a rational explanation for his experience. Most humans have no knowledge of the presence of aliens or the capabilities of their technology,' Mr Monk agreed.

Alfie thought about that for a moment. Most humans? He wasn't the only one then? Presence of aliens? There were others, on Earth? Just like always, the more he learnt, the more he realized that he didn't know. Focus, he mouthed again, getting comfortable in the pilot's chair.

'So! The Variado isn't Mr Sloan any more. The trouble is, that I don't know who or where he is,' Alfie explained.

'Would you like me to perform a location scan for Variado life signs?' Mr Monk offered.

'Yes, please,' Alfie replied, focusing on the screen and wondering what it would show this time.

First there was the whole of Earth, the globe slowly spinning. It didn't look like most maps. It didn't show the borders of countries; it wasn't colour-coded depending on who controlled that area. It showed the land in shades of green and brown, with blue for oceans. As expected the globe settled on Europe and the screen was soon filled with the United Kingdom.

Alfie leaned forward eagerly as the map zoomed in on his village, familiar street names showing up. Even so, he stared in shock for a few moments, his brain refusing to take in where the red dot was. Of all the places in the world that Alfie should have thought to look for the Variado, it was there. Of course it was. It was the perfect place to get him alone, the perfect place to lay an ambush.

His home.

Twenty-five

Alfie stared. The world span and his stomach did somersaults. He blinked and squinted, hoping the red dot on the map would move, but it stayed where it was. No matter how much he might want it to be otherwise, the sensors were telling him the Variado was right in the middle of his house. Mum! Lizzie!

Alfie threw himself out of the seat and back towards the transport hub, yelling 'RETURN!' as he ran and sucking in a breath to last him through the journey back to the alley.

As soon as he felt solid pavement under his feet, he started running, ignoring a startled Amy who shrieked when he appeared right next to her in a rush of air and static.

'Alfie! Stop!' she yelled, running after him. 'What is it?'

'It's at my HOUSE!'

Alfie was sprinting fast enough now that Amy was struggling to keep up with him. His PE teacher had been right then – all he needed was the right motivation and he could run faster than anyone!

'Alfie, wait!' Amy shouted again. 'You can't just go

running in there! What are you going to do?'

Alfie didn't care. He finally understood the expression "couldn't see straight" because the world looked all red and jumpy. The only thing he could think about was his family. If the Variado had hurt them at all, he didn't know what he would do.

Amy was just a second behind him as he sprinted up the drive and burst through the door yelling, 'MUM!'

Her voice came from the front room, almost straight away.

'In here, Alfie.'

With his heart banging like a bass drum in his ears and his breathing so noisy from running and panic, Alfie couldn't tell if she sounded normal or not.

Amy grabbed his hand, pulling him back and behind her so she walked into the living room first. She stood in the door frame with both hands out, blocking Alfie from getting in.

'Hello, Mrs S,' she greeted.

'Oh, Amy! You're here too. Come on in. Alfie. Shut the front door, would you?'

Alfie did just that, following Amy as she walked into the living room.

Alfie looked desperately around the room for any sign of trouble but everything looked just how he remembered it. No alien blobs, no signs of a struggle, nothing unexpected.

Mum was sat in her usual chair, a cup of tea on the table in front of her. Lizzie was playing with her stuffed animals. Vets, Alfie thought, noticing she was wearing a white hat with a red cross on the top. There was no sign of the Variado, no sign that anything was wrong. Mum and Lizzie were…well, Mum and Lizzie.

'About time you got here, Alfie. I was expecting you about fifteen minutes ago!' Mum chided.

'Yeah, sorry. I had to go to Amy's after dance,' Alfie explained, his chest still working hard. He couldn't stop looking around him for the Variado. He knew it had to be there, but where? If it wasn't disguised as Mum or Lizzie, had it taken the place of a piece of furniture or something? Did the coffee table look suspicious?

Glancing at Amy, he saw that same worried look on her face that she'd had in the alley. She was doubting him again. How could she when he'd been to the *Monkesto* and back right in front of her!

'Mrs Slider. Can I talk to you?' Amy asked, and Alfie knew what was going to happen next. Amy was going to tell his mum that she thought Alfie was mental.

'Well, now isn't the best time,' Alfie's mum replied, 'Maybe in a little while. Alfie, there's someone here to see you.'

Alfie had the satisfaction of seeing Amy's eyes go wide as she realized that the Variado might be here after all.

He gave her an "I told you so" look before focusing on his mum. 'Oh?'

Sensing movement behind him, Alfie turned to see a harmless looking old lady walk into the room. She had silver hair that was set solid into a fluffy "do". She was wearing a smart dress covered with a warm cardigan that looked like it was hand knitted, and very shiny shoes. She looked harmless, that is, until you looked her in the eyes. Hard, cold eyes looked out from the doughy face of the old lady. The Variado! It had to be.

Alfie and Amy both took a big step back to let it past, as it bustled into the room, moving a bit too steadily for an old lady.

'This is Mrs Chieveley,' Mum explained as the Variado walked to an empty chair and sat down.

Alfie watched as it picked up a cup of tea and took a sip, those strange, dark eyes watching Alfie over the rim.

'It was Mrs Chieveley's key that you found. She's been waiting for you to bring it back,' Mum said.

'Oh,' said Alfie. He concentrated very hard on not putting his hand in his pocket to hold the key.

'OK. Ummm…' Alfie knew he had to say something, to take control. Under pressure his brain was just short-circuiting.

'Alfie left it at school,' Amy piped up. Alfie wondered how he was going to repay Amy for just stepping up like that.

'Umm, yeah. It's in my locker at school,' Alfie agreed. 'I can't get it until tomorrow.'

The alien peered across the brim of the teacup at him, 'Now.'

'Oh, well he can't get it now,' Mum saved his skin this time, even if she didn't know it. 'School is all locked up. It'll have to be after school tomorrow.'

The Variado said nothing; it just stared across at Alfie, hardly blinking. Like a lizard, Alfie thought.

Alfie cleared his throat. Out of the corner of his eye he could see Mum sitting forward, her forehead creasing as she realized something was a bit off.

'The thing is,' Alfie said slowly, picking his words with care, 'the shed that it opens is pretty smashed up. Some of what's inside is alright, though.'

'So, after school,' Amy said, sounding completely confident. 'We'll collect up everything that didn't get damaged and bring it to you? We'll take away your recycling at the same time.'

Alfie shot Amy a quick smile. Brilliant! She'd just told the Variado that they would give it the cargo, in return for the real Mrs Chieveley. At least, he hoped the alien had understood that.

The Variado nodded, standing up a bit unsteadily just like any old lady except for those eyes. Awful, flat, emotionless eyes.

'After school tomorrow. At Parker's Field.'

Alfie knew the place, a big bit of land that had been too damp to build on. It wasn't far from school. He tried to fill his voice with confidence, like a hero in a film, like someone who wouldn't take any nonsense. 'That's fine. We can all get what we need.'

The old lady nodded, then without another word walked out of the house. Alfie and Amy both stepped well back again to let the alien past. They shared a look, scared, excited, pleased with themselves.

'Well! What a strange lady!' Mum said, once she'd followed the Variado out and closed the door behind it. Alfie heard the key turning in the lock, something Mum only did if she was feeling worried. 'You *are* lovely kids, helping her with her chores.'

Alfie grinned at Amy. He was starting to get used to how Mum would fill in the blanks and explain things away so they made sense. The less he told her, the easier it seemed for her to make up her own explanation.

'Now, what did you need to talk to me about Amy?' Mum asked.

Amy shook her head, 'Oh, yeah! I just wanted to ask if Alfie could come around to my house after school tomorrow.'

Alfie had to admit it; Amy was a way better liar than he was!

'Ah, well that's fine. Of course he can.' Mum smiled and bustled off to make dinner.

Alfie let out a big sigh. It was going to be OK. This time tomorrow, it would all be over.

Twenty-Six

With the door closed and locked behind the alien, Alfie let his relief turn into a hug with Amy. As his arms wrapped around her, he could feel her shaking. He caught her eye and gave her a smile he hoped would reassure her. They'd faced the alien!

The relief didn't last long though. It was soon replaced with worries about how they were going to handle the exchange tomorrow. Realizing they needed time to plan, Alfie asked his mum if Amy could stay for tea. After they'd eaten, they told his parents they needed to work on a project in the dining room so they could talk without being interrupted.

Alfie spread some paper out on the table so it looked like they were working, sat back in his chair and said, 'You were amazing then. With the Variado, I mean. Really quick thinking.'

'Someone had to,' Amy replied. She was smiling at the compliment but it wasn't going to stop her taking the mickey out of Alfie.

'Yeah, well. You try having an evil alien in the room with *your* family and see how you feel.'

Amy nodded. Even thinking about it took the sparkle from her eyes.

'So, how do we do this? How do we outsmart it?' she asked.

Alfie sighed. 'I don't know. It's dangerous. We need to convince it that the ship is no good, that the cops are on their way and that we're giving it something more valuable than a box of frogs.'

'Yeah,' Amy agreed. 'And we need to make sure that we have the real Mrs Chieveley back before we give it *anything*.'

Alfie simply nodded, his brain was usually full of good ideas but right now he was running on empty.

'You said the Variado doesn't know what's on the ship?' Amy pointed out.

Alfie nodded again, 'Mr Monk says it shouldn't know. It probably won't be happy with fire-farting frogs, though.'

He couldn't quite keep the giggle out of his voice as he said that. Alfie saw that Amy was pressing her lips tightly together to hold her own laughter in. Then neither of them could stop it. The giggles spilled out, like bubbles from lemonade that's been given a good shake.

It felt good to just laugh and be silly, like kids should be. Alfie was beginning to relax when Amy's expression changed. She gasped, the smile morphing into a more serious expression.

'Alfie.' When he didn't stop laughing she leaned over and slapped him on the arm. 'Alfie! I've got an idea!'

Alfie winced, rubbing his arm as he grumbled, 'What?'

'You said the frogs are only dangerous if they've eaten something special, right? What was it?'

'Erm. Phenol?'

'Right. So, I'm betting that those frogs don't have any phenol in there with them *now*. But what if they did?' Amy said.

'If they did…then when the Variado opened the crate, the frogs would all fart fire,' Alfie enjoyed saying that.

'Exactly! That would give it a fright, and it'd be too busy with fire alarms and stuff to worry about us. It would just want to get away, before the Skolto Service came.'

Alfie's smile got wider as he worked out what Amy was thinking, 'You know that might just work! Be more trouble than it's worth to it!' He thought for a moment, then asked, 'But where do we get phenol from?'

Amy nodded over towards the computer, on a desk in the corner of the room, 'Don't ask me, ask Google.'

Alfie did just that, jumping into the swivel chair and quickly pulling up the search engine and typing in "Where can I get phenol".

Clicking on the first link, Alfie found himself on a page about Public Health. Most of it didn't make sense to him, but it did say that phenol was used in some medicines. He searched again, this time for "Phenol Medicine" but all he got was throat sprays.

'I'm not squirting spray down a frog's throat!' he exclaimed.

Just then his mum came in with a tray. On it were two glasses of milk and a couple of chocolate chip cookies. Alfie mumbled his thanks, and joined Amy at the table, feeling defeated.

'What's up?' Mum asked, picking up on their mood.

'We need some phenol,' Alfie said, 'For our project.'

'Hmmm. We don't have any but Granny might,' Mum said.

'She might?' Alfie asked. 'Why would Granny have phenol?'

'It's used in some antiseptic creams. I don't like the smell, but I think it's the kind Granny has.'

Alfie looked at Amy. Amy lifted an eyebrow, a hopeful spark in her eyes.

'That's awesome. Thanks, Mum!'

'Any time,' she replied as she shut the door behind her.

'I can go to Granny's on the way to school and get her cream,' Alfie said, 'then just squeeze a bit in with the frogs…'

'Without them escaping,' Amy cautioned.

'Oh. Yeah,' Alfie pulled a face, 'and I have to do it quickly because they can't be in the air when they eat it…'

'Or else it will be you that gets burnt,' Amy agreed.

Alfie cleared his throat nervously. Well, they had a plan. It seemed like a good one, but there was still a lot that could go wrong. He'd need to be on the ball tomorrow!

Twenty-Seven

The alarm rang, and Alfie groaned. He'd set it for an hour early, so he had time to go to Granny's for the antiseptic and then the *Monkesto* to set the trap on his way to school. The trouble was, he'd been so worried, going over and over the ideas that he and Amy had come up with the day before that he had found it really hard to get to sleep.

He wasn't sure what time it was when he'd finally drifted off, but he'd dreamed about knocking over frog tanks and his head felt all foggy and slow.

As soon as his brain made the connection with what today was, and what they had to do, he sat bolt upright like an electric shock had gone through him. Today was the day that he would either sort this whole mess out, or he would…well, best not to think about that.

He dressed quickly, grabbed the school bag he'd packed the night before and went quietly downstairs.

He had been hoping that he could just sneak out without anyone noticing. He didn't want to say goodbye when he wasn't sure if he was going to make it back.

There were noises coming from the kitchen though,

and as he peered around the corner he saw Mum and Dad both in there. Dad was filling a travel mug with coffee to take to work with him. Mum was just stood looking bleary-eyed, wearing her dressing gown and nursing her own mug. Alfie felt a big surge of love for them, quickly followed by the sour taste of fear as he realized if today went wrong, this might be the last time he saw them.

Mum noticed him, her sleepy expression clearing into a smile as she put her mug down and held out her arms for a hug.

Alfie wasn't sure he could cope with that. He thought that if she hugged him then he might never want her to stop. He waved his packed bags at her instead. 'I've got to go. You know, that project?'

Mum nodded, but she walked towards him anyway. She ran a hand down his cheek, cupped his chin and looked into his eyes. 'Love you,' she said simply.

She said it a lot, it wasn't unusual, but hearing it today made hot tears prickle at Alfie's eyes.

'I know,' he replied, pulling away from her touch. 'I love you too.'

Alfie couldn't quite meet her eye as he turned and slipped out of the house. He couldn't look back. He knew that he just had to keep moving forward, it was more important than just him missing his mum. The whole planet was at risk.

His granny lived on the other side of the village, but it wasn't a big place so it would only take him five minutes to get there on his bike. He couldn't afford to waste a minute. He had a lot to do and he didn't want to be late for school.

He was bang on time when he got to Granny's, abandoning his bike on her drive and knocking on the door before he walked in. Granny's door was always open if she was awake, no matter how many times Dad told her she shouldn't leave it like that.

'Granny?' he called, letting himself into the front room.

Granny was sat on the sofa in front of the TV. She was watching one of her favourite quiz programmes.

'Amsterdam!' she shouted, then turned to him and said, 'Morning, Alfie. Mum said you might come.'

'Yes, I wondered if you had any—' Alfie stopped as Granny waved a hand at him. The quizmaster was asking another question and she wanted to listen.

'A caravan is a group of which animals?' came the voice from the TV.

'Camels,' Granny said, with certainty.

'Horses?' guessed the contestant.

Granny doubled up with laughter. 'Horses!' she gasped. 'Honestly, what do they teach them in schools these days?'

Alfie looked at the woman on the screen, who must be about fifty. He didn't think it was fair to still be blaming school for what she didn't know.

'Granny...' he began again, only to be waved into silence.

'The correct answer is...' the quizmaster announced, leaving an annoyingly long gap before he finished, '...camels!'

'Ha! Told you!' Granny celebrated.

Alfie realized he would have to wait until the adverts to talk to his gran and sat down on the sofa beside her.

He tapped his foot anxiously as he watched the clock. He didn't have time for this!

Granny had a table in front of her, and it always had biscuits and sweets on it. Alfie helped himself to a ginger nut as he watched the quiz and waited for the commercial break. Just when he was about to give up and go in search of Granny's first aid kit for himself, the show theme tune played and the credits rolled.

'Now then!' Granny said, turning to Alfie. 'Your mum said you wanted some antiseptic cream. Have you been hurting yourself?'

'No, Gran,' Alfie reassured her, 'it's for a science project.'

'Oh! That's good. Science is good. I'm glad your school is teaching you things like science. I don't want to see you on a quiz show saying that a group of horses is a caravan!'

Alfie nodded, he didn't think he was likely to forget it was camels.

'Gran, I'm going to be late if I don't get the cream. I have to go.'

'Oh!' Granny looked disappointed and Alfie chewed his lip at the guilty feeling in his stomach. He knew that Granny got lonely and loved having some company.

'I'll come and see you at the weekend?' he promised. 'Tell you how the science project went?'

Granny nodded, 'Alright, sweetheart. Now, let me see where I've put the cream.'

Alfie waited while Granny got up and tottered into her kitchen. He grabbed another ginger nut, as he was feeling a bit queasy with nerves and ginger was supposed to be good for stomachs.

He could hear Granny rummaging around in cupboards and muttering. Alfie looked at the clock and sighed. He was going to have to cycle at top speed to get back to the *Monkesto*. He'd been here ten minutes already.

Finally, Granny emerged with a tube that she waved towards Alfie.

He took it from her and looked on the back, smiling as he read the first ingredient. Phenol.

'Fantastic, Gran, thank you!' Alfie hopped up and wrapped her in a big hug, 'You're amazing. I've got to rush off now but I'll be back at the weekend.'

'Will you? Good lad. Just like your dad.' Gran said as she sat back down on the sofa.

Her timing was perfect. The quiz show theme was playing again.

'Welcome back! Just before the break we saw...'

Alfie smiled, watching Gran get absorbed in the quiz again.

'Bye,' he said, but she didn't answer. Mum would tell me off if I forgot my manners like that, Alfie thought with a smile.

Grabbing Granny's front door keys from the hook as he left, Alfie locked the door and posted them back through. He loved his Gran, and she needed to be safe. Didn't she know there were evil shape-shifting aliens around!

Twenty-Eight

The streets were quiet at that time of the morning. It was like being in a secret world, Alfie thought, before most people were up and about. The only sounds were adults leaving their houses and getting into their cars to drive to work. No shouting kids, no rumble of scooter wheels, no dogs barking out warnings to passing children.

It felt like everything was more real than usual, like Alfie was seeing it in high definition. The birds tweeting sounded like conversation, not random noise. He realized he was noticing things that he would usually ignore, a scrap of litter here, a bit of graffiti there. Someone was having bacon for breakfast, and the smell teased Alfie's stomach as he approached the knothole. How ordinary, he thought.

Leaning his bike against the fence, Alfie stood for a minute, eyes closed and hand grasping the key, steadying himself for the trip to the *Monkesto*.

Seconds later and he was stepping off the red dot and walking to the pilot's seat, making himself comfortable as the system came to life.

'Mr Monk, we have a plan,' he began. 'The Variado is

disguised as an old lady called Mrs Chieveley. Is the real old lady on its ship, in suspended animation?'

The screen showed the usual map, zooming in on the area where they had discovered the Variado's ship before, when Mr Sloan was on it.

'There is a human life sign at that location, consistent with being in suspended animation.'

Alfie let out a breath in relief; Mrs Chieveley was alive.

'Alright, so here's the plan. We're going to meet with the Variado after school. We're going to make it give us back the old lady, and we're going to give him the frogs. How can we do that? How can we make sure that the crate only gets there when we want it to?'

'Alfie Slider, you are using the word "we". Who are you referring to?' Mr Monk asked.

Alfie's cheeks felt suddenly hot, just as his stomach felt like ice. It was like the time he'd confidently gone to the front of the class to give his answer, got his words in a muddle and accidentally said a swear word. The *Monkesto* was supposed to be top secret and he'd blabbed the whole story to Amy. How much trouble was he going to be in?

Should he lie? Alfie wondered. Was there a story that he could make up that would explain what he'd just said as a slip of the tongue? No, he thought, this is too important. I need to tell the truth. 'My friend, Amy Rodgers.'

It seemed like there was a long silence, where Alfie picked at his fingernails anxiously. He was expecting Mr Monk to tell him off, tell him about breaking protocols or something, but instead the silence just stretched on and on.

'Um. Amy is cool, and smart,' Alfie continued. 'I didn't want to get her involved because I know it's dangerous, but I needed her help.'

Silence continued for a few more beats of Alfie's tense heart before the computer spoke, 'The safest option would be to reprogram your access device to work as a remote control for the transportation system.'

Alfie took a moment to get over his surprise that the computer had just accepted Amy being involved. Then it took another moment to work through all those big words.

'Umm, you mean that I could use the key? I press a button or something and the crate arrives?'

'Yes,' Mr Monk replied. 'Place the access device on the console for reprogramming.' As it spoke part of the console slid back, and another piece, like a tray, came out.

Alfie got the key from his pocket and held it in his hand, weighing it up. Could he trust Mr Monk? He knew the computer wanted to keep the *Monkesto* safe more than anything else. What if it just took the key away and kept Alfie a prisoner? If Alfie was trapped here, its problems were over. What if it was actually angry that he'd involved Amy? What if doing that had broken some rules or something, so Alfie couldn't be trusted any more?

'Do you think it's a good plan?' Alfie asked, fingers closing around the key.

'It is not without danger, Alfie Slider. The safest course of action would be to wait until the Skolto Service come in search of this vessel, but as you have said, you and your family are in danger.'

Alfie started breathing again; he hadn't even realized he'd been holding his breath until he did. He nodded.

'Yes. Thank you. That's the most important thing, right? Keeping people safe.'

'The oath which officers of the Skolto Service take includes the words "protect the innocent",' Mr Monk replied. 'This plan is consistent with that ideal.'

Alfie hesitated. He still wasn't completely sure he could trust the computer, but he didn't see what choice he had. He put the key into the tray and watched as it was pulled back inside the console. He rubbed his belly, a nagging ache in his guts telling him that things weren't right. There was nothing he could do now but wait. In a few minutes he'd know, one way or another.

Twenty-Nine

A big part of Alfie wanted to just sit and stare at the console until the key popped back out, but he knew he couldn't. He had too much to do. Rummaging in the backpack he found the tube of antiseptic and pulled it out.

'I'm going to set the frog trap,' he told Mr Monk. He got no answer, as usual. He hadn't asked a question and the computer didn't give out information unless he did.

Mr Monk was definitely paying attention though, as the doors that needed to be opened and closed as Alfie moved from the cockpit to that strange, in between room and then on to the cargo bay, all did so without him needing to ask.

'Mr Monk, please open the crate containing the frogs,' Alfie asked, focusing his attention on the shining silvery crate in front of him.

The only response was a clicking sound from the crate. Alfie watched as a cloud of white steam or smoke found its way out from the gap where the seal had broken and started pouring down the sides.

The lid looked heavy. Alfie put down the tube of cream to use both hands to push it up, but actually he could have done it with a little finger. As soon as he pushed with even a tiny amount of force, the lid swung smoothly open.

Alfie's lips formed a perfect O in surprise. The lid was hinged on the opposite side of the crate and Alfie found he was looking down onto the top of three tanks, surrounded on all sides by the white gas. It hung heavy in the air. Like dry ice, Alfie thought, but it smells like a swimming pool.

He was so focused on the crate that he jumped when Mr Monk broke the silence.

'Change in crate conditions will allow the frogs to wake from sedation in approximately ten seconds.'

'Great! That might have been helpful to know *before* I opened the crate!' Alfie complained, but he didn't have time to waste on arguing.

In front of him were three tanks, each with a lid. He needed to pull those off, squirt in some cream and then slam the lid down on the crate before ten seconds was up. Well, probably more like seven now.

Not wasting any more time, he started moving, pleased to find that the lids came off the tanks easily. He threw the first one away and was reaching for the second when he caught sight of one of the frogs and let out a little shriek. He was glad no one had been around to hear *that*.

The frog was much bigger than he'd expected, about the size of his head, hunched down in the bottom of the tank. Alfie stared at the first one, even as he was pulling the lids off the second and third tanks. Its skin was slimy and shiny, like you'd expect, but it rippled and swirled with rainbow colours, like disco lights. It was almost hypnotic.

Pulling himself together, Alfie grabbed the tube, and tried to get the top off. It was stuck. Growling in frustration, Alfie twisted hard, going red in the face, until it started to move.

Oh, the smell! He agreed with Mum – it was horrible. It reminded Alfie of the dentist's. Pulling a face as it tickled his nostrils, he quickly squirted what was left in the tube, dividing it between the three tanks.

How long was that then? Three seconds left? Bags of time! He reached up for the lid, still staring at the frog, but his hand just found air. He had to look away from the frog to guide his hand back to the lid. His fingers had just made contact when there was a loud "rrrrribiit"!

Panic set in as Alfie looked down to see the first frog had opened its large eyes. They shone and shimmered in red and gold, like molten metal. Its tongue shot out and dived into the cream.

'Aaaargh!' Alfie screeched, slamming the lid closed in panic.

Heart thudding, Alfie backed away from the frog crate quickly, startling himself by bumping against the other one. The unknown cargo.

He turned to face it, looking over the identical, shimmering silver surface. He didn't have time to wonder what was in there right now; he had an alien to outsmart. Breathing heavily, Alfie walked away, out of the cargo bay and back towards the cockpit. The trap was set!

'Mr Monk?' Alfie called as he walked back towards the pilot's chair, 'Are you angry with me, for telling Amy?'

The computer's voice responded quickly this time, 'Computers do not feel emotion, Alfie Slider. I have been programmed to understand emotion in others, and to modulate my voice to support the operator of this vessel, but I am not capable of anger.' The voice sounded like it was full of understanding and kindness. Alfie couldn't believe that was just good programming.

Alfie shook his head; a voice in it kept telling him there was more going on. Mr Monk continued to speak, 'You are not an employee of the Skolto Service and are not bound by its laws. Your actions so far have been intelligent and responsible.'

Alfie let out a breath, letting go of the tension that he'd been holding. OK, so he wasn't in trouble then? Good. As if to prove it, the panel on the console opened and the tray containing the key slid out. Alfie grabbed it quickly, just in case.

'The access device has been reprogrammed to allow remote commands to be issued to this vessel,' Mr Monk explained.

Alfie closed his hand around the key. It had been the thing that had got him into this mess in the first place, now it was going to be the thing that got him out of it.

Thirty

As he cycled to school, Alfie had the weird feeling that he was out of synch with everyone else. All around him people were acting like it was a normal day, which it was for them, but not for Alfie! He'd just been to a parallel universe to set a trap, to deal with a shape-changing alien that was trying to steal a spaceship. Oh, and anyone else knowing about any of that could be a danger to the whole planet!

Mums were telling their kids off for walking in puddles, or dropping their school bags. Kids were saying they felt sick and didn't want to go to school. A group of boys from Alfie's year walked past, heads close together as they looked at the latest gaming magazine.

Alfie wanted to scream at everyone, to tell them to wake up! He wanted to shout, right in their faces, 'There are aliens around us!' The universe was so much more complicated than people thought, but he was the only one who knew.

Then his eyes flitted over a familiar face and he remembered. He wasn't the only one; there was Amy. She was stood by the bike sheds with her arms crossed, standing very still, very stiff, like she needed to hug herself for reassurance.

Alfie flashed her a smile, happy all over again that he had someone with him on this adventure, that he wasn't alone.

'It's all sorted. I got the antiseptic and fed the frogs. Those things are HUGE!'

Amy managed a half smile back, but it didn't make her look any less nervous. That made Alfie nervous too. Had she thought of something overnight that he hadn't?

'You alright, Ames?' he asked as he drew alongside her.

'Yeah,' she answered, but Alfie could hear a little quiver in her voice. 'No. Not really,' she admitted. 'It's just weird, being in school when we have something so important to do. I feel like we deserve a day off for this, really.'

Alfie laughed, 'Yeah. Shall we ask Miss Beavis? Or wait 'til tomorrow after it's all done and things are back to normal.'

Amy glanced at Alfie, then started walking, 'Do you think things are ever going to get back to normal?'

Alfie's eyebrows shot up in surprise, 'Umm. Yes? Once the Variado has gone, then things will be pretty normal.'

'You'll still have the key. You'll still be the one who has to keep the *Monkesto* safe,' Amy countered.

Alfie felt like a weight settled over him as he realized Amy was right. This wasn't going to be over today, but at least the danger would be. Anger bubbled up inside that Amy had given him something else to worry about. Today was difficult enough as it was.

'Well, we can think about that once we've stopped the alien from threatening my family!' Alfie grumbled, he knew that he wasn't really being fair, but he couldn't stop himself.

Amy nodded, falling silent as they walked together into school.

Alfie felt like he was bubbling inside. It was almost impossible to concentrate. School could be boring at times anyway, but there was so much on his mind today. He literally had the weight of the world on his shoulders, so did times tables really matter? Amy was right. Normal wasn't an option anymore, but once the Variado had been dealt with there could be a new normal. A new normal where Alfie had his own spaceship! He wondered what sort of calculations the *Monkesto*'s computer could manage. He was sure Mr Monk wouldn't struggle with what six times seven was.

A part of him realized that at some point the Skolto Service would probably come looking for the *Monkesto* but, until then, it was all his.

His whole day was like a ride on a roller coaster. Big bursts of excitement thinking that the Variado would soon be gone, that the new normal could begin, then uhoh! Super-fast sinking of the stomach when he remembered what he had to pull off to get to that part.

Alfie could see from the way Amy was twitching and running her hands in her hair that she was feeling the same way too. He tried a few times to talk to her about it, but Amy wasn't meeting his eye or she'd walk off just as he got close. He decided after a while that she was doing it deliberately, she just didn't want to talk about it.

In spite of that, she was right by his side in the line to go out at 3.25 pm. Alfie was struggling to put that day's letters into his school bag, and she calmly took them out of his hand, folded them and slid them into a gap that he hadn't even noticed. She kept looking right into his eyes, and Alfie thought she was trying to let him know that she understood. He was so glad that she was going to be with him for this last part.

They left together, every step making Alfie feel more and more queasy as they moved further from school and turned down the alley that would lead them to Parker's Field.

Alfie heard Amy let out a big sigh, and he wanted to say something to comfort her but he had no idea what. Instead he just kept quiet.

Soon they were walking down the alley that lead to the field, and zigzagging around the bollards at the end. They stepped out onto the wide green space known as Parker's Field.

It was a big square of grass. Houses backed onto it around three sides, but the fence at the back looked out into the farm that bordered the village. The most obvious thing to Alfie was that the field was empty. There was no sign at all of an alien spaceship.

'It's not here,' Amy whispered, then said more loudly, 'Where is it?'

Alfie shrugged. He had no idea; he just kept looking around the field for any sign of the Variado. There was only one way in, an uncomfortable thought informed him, and it was behind them. Spinning around quickly, Alfie expected to see the Variado in the alley, ready to ambush them, but it was empty.

'Weird,' he muttered. Where was the Variado? What was the pirate alien up to now?

Thirty-One

Amy took another step forward, made a high-pitched squealing noise and jumped back.

'What's that?' she pointed at the air just in front of her as she rubbed her nose with the other hand.

'What?' Alfie asked. 'There's nothing there.'

'Nothing you can *see*,' Amy replied, but as she carefully moved forward Alfie could see that her hair was being pulled forwards in a cloud around her face, like if you rub a balloon on your head.

'Static electricity?' Alfie asked, taking a step forward himself and feeling a sort of buzzing, fizzing sensation as he did, 'A force field?' He had no idea, really, but it sounded like something an alien ship might have, and it was a lot better than saying nothing.

'You think the Variado's ship is here?' Amy asked. Then, almost as if it were an answer to her question, there was a loud hissing noise. The air in front of them wavered like a heat haze, and through it Alfie could see the Variado's ship. Then the haze disappeared and the ship was there, just as it always had been, but visible.

It wasn't that big – about the same size and shape

as a bus. That surprised Alfie, as he'd imagined that it would be a saucer shape, like the *Monkesto*, or sleek like the ships in TV shows. He didn't have time to take in the details of the craft because, with a hiss of air, a ramp opened up in the centre with two identical figures standing on it.

Two old ladies, stood side by side, like mirror images. The same height, same build, and dressed in the same clothes.

Alfie turned to look at Amy and saw her mouth had dropped open. He had a moment to think about how this was the first time she'd really seen anything "out of this world" and then one of the old ladies spoke.

'Give me the access device.'

As soon as it spoke Alfie realized that the one on the right must be the Variado. Both Mrs Chieveleys came to a stop at exactly the same time.

'There's no point. The ship is wrecked,' Alfie replied. 'It sent off a distress signal. The owners are on their way. All I can give you is the cargo, but that's the best part anyway.'

The Variado paused, just staring right at Alfie.

'You know I'm telling the truth! You shot the ship down. Look, I'm just a human. I don't know or care about all this stuff, so just take the cargo and go. The ship's not worth having, really. It's toast.'

The alien continued to stare; it wasn't even blinking. Alfie felt like he was being scanned by beams that got heavier with every passing second. 'The Skolto Service are on their way. They'll be here really soon. You could always talk to them about it…'

'What is in the crate?' the Variado asked.

'I don't know, some sort of weapon,' Alfie said, hoping he could pull off a half lie. 'Give us the old lady, and I'll transport it to you.' He paused, then added, 'You shouldn't hang around here. The Skolto Service...'

'Give me the cargo.'

'When Mrs Chieveley is safely off the ship,' Alfie replied, doing his best to sound like he wasn't going to take any nonsense.

'You can see she is safe,' the Variado countered.

Alfie swallowed. It was true. He could see the old lady and she seemed fine. She wasn't speaking, she was just stood there, looking a bit worried. Then she coughed, so quietly it made no noise. She covered her mouth with her hand.

'Mrs Chieveley, are you alright?' Alfie asked.

There was no reply from the old lady.

Alfie cast a sideways look at Amy. He had a bad feeling about this. Why wasn't the old lady saying anything? Why was she just stood there?

'Mrs Chieveley?' As Alfie spoke, the old lady coughed again.

There was something about that which bothered Alfie but he tried to push the thought out of his mind so he could concentrate on the Variado.

'Transport the cargo,' the Variado spoke again. Alfie had never felt so uneasy in his life. He had an old lady's life literally in the palm of his hand! 'Transport the cargo, or I will destroy you all!'

Alfie stared at the alien, mouth open. Was the Variado serious? Alfie swallowed, his mind racing as he tried to decide what to do.

'Alfie,' Amy hissed.

'What?' he grumbled, not wanting to be distracted.

'Mrs Chieveley keeps coughing,' Amy replied.

'Uhuh...' Alfie wasn't really listening, that didn't seem too important right now.

'I mean...I don't think it's her. It's like a recording or something,' Amy replied.

Alfie squinted then, looking more closely at the other Mrs Chieveley. Amy was right, she didn't look quite real, and as he watched she did exactly the same cough again. Tilting his head to one side, Alfie looked more closely. As soon as the Variado noticed, it screeched 'Transport the cargo NOW!'

'No,' Alfie said, reaching for Amy's hand and taking a step back. 'That isn't Mrs Chieveley. Give us the real old lady or you get nothing.' His certainty grew as the old lady coughed again, like a 3D video playing on a loop.

The Variado made a horrible, rasping, frustrated noise and the world shimmered in front of them until the ship and its ramp were hidden from view again.

Alfie glanced at Amy; she looked just as sick and terrified as he felt. Had they just made the biggest mistake of their lives? Had they just killed Mrs Chieveley?

Thirty-Two

Alfie doubled over, it felt like he'd been punched in the stomach. Shaking his head as he tried not to bring up his lunch on the green grass, he thought he'd never felt so ill in his whole life.

'Oh no,' Amy moaned beside him. 'Oh no. What did we just do?'

Alfie looked at Amy, and saw his own feelings mirrored on her face. She was pale and had her mouth open like she couldn't get enough air. She looked as scared as he felt.

'We should, uh, go,' Alfie whispered, 'before it fires up its weapons or whatever.'

'Yeah!' Amy agreed, tensing up at the thought of weapons.

They were just about to run when the world shimmered again and with the same hissing noise the ramp of the Variado's ship came into view.

If you didn't know any better, an old lady was walking towards you carrying another old lady. Alfie knew better, and he stared anxiously at the real Mrs Chieveley who was limp in the alien's arms. He was trying to work out if she was alright.

The Variado stopped halfway and said, 'You can see her. Show me the cargo.'

Alfie's knees turned to marshmallow. He had to lock them to stay upright. The relief! Mrs Chieveley wasn't moving, but from what he could see she was asleep, not dead. Alfie straightened up, took a breath to collect himself and nodded. He didn't trust the Variado, so without taking the key from his pocket and revealing it to the alien he said, 'Transport the cargo to my location.'

The breezy, tingling feeling behind him let Alfie know the crate had arrived from the *Monkesto*. He resisted the urge to turn and check; he thought it would look cooler if he didn't. He wanted the Variado to think it was dealing with a hero.

'Give us Mrs Chieveley and you can have the cargo,' Alfie said firmly.

There was a long moment when the Variado just continued to stare, and Alfie worried it wasn't going to do what he'd asked. Then it took three more steps and bent down and rolled the old lady down off the ramp onto the damp grass like she was a bag of rubbish.

'Hey!' Alfie could hear the anger vibrating in Amy's voice. He hoped that she would realize she needed to calm down, because he didn't want to take his eyes off the double-crossing shape-shifter. He trusted Amy to make sure the old lady was alright.

'You take this cargo and leave this planet,' Alfie said, trying to sound like a character in one of his mum's favourite shows. 'There's nothing else for you here.'

'This is a backwards planet,' the Variado hissed. 'Give me the cargo.'

Alfie glanced down to Amy, watching his friend check Mrs Chieveley's pulse. He waited until she nodded to say the old lady was alright, before he said, 'Transport the cargo to the Variado's vessel. Give it access to unlock the crate.'

Alfie's hair was ruffled by the rapid burst of air that accompanied the transportation. The Variado made a weird series of clicks and whistles, then listened to some similar noises that came from a speaker on a panel nearby. It turned and walked into its ship without a backward glance. Alfie blinked in astonishment as it transformed from the shape of the old lady into a black, formless shadow. One second it was a human, the next it oozed out of shape like an oil spill. Alfie filed the experience away for later. He was too scared to enjoy the coolness of it right now.

The ramp closed up and he heard the roar of engines starting up. The force field, or whatever it was, shimmered back into place, and hid the Variado and its ship from sight. Alfie ran to Amy's side.

'Is she alright?' he asked, dropping to his knees by the old lady.

'I think so,' Amy replied, and even as she said that, Mrs Chieveley opened her eyes.

'Oh, hello!' Amy greeted her. 'Are you alright? We just found you lying here, on the grass.'

Alfie had to admit it, Amy was much better at covering up than he was.

'I...oh,' Mrs Chieveley glanced around her, confused. 'Where am I?'

Amy and Alfie helped her to her feet, the increasing

noise from the engines told them they needed to move quickly. Alfie let Amy do the talking. He just knew they needed to get out of the place before Mrs Chieveley asked where the engine noise was coming from.

Alfie had expected it to be hot behind them, perhaps for them even to have been burnt by the blast off, but it was nothing like that. It was the strangest sensation he had ever felt. It was like everything, every part of his body, every cell, was quivering. It was really unpleasant. This is what it must feel like to be a jelly, Alfie thought.

The earth vibrated beneath their feet as they helped the old lady away. The noise was almost deafening and if she did ask any questions about it, her words were drowned out.

It was only from the direction of the sound that you could tell that the ship was lifting off, heading up into the sky. The further away it went, the less noticeable that horrible quivering feeling was.

They were more than halfway down the alley, the noise level was more like a helicopter going over, and the quivering was hardly noticeable. Alfie let out a sigh of relief, sharing a smile with Amy. It had all come right in the end, hadn't it?

That's when the world exploded around them.

Thirty-Three

The noise was so loud it felt like a physical blow; a tremendous crashing, tearing sound, as though the sky was being split in two. Alfie didn't want to turn his head to look; his brain was just helpfully providing an image of a massive lightning bolt headed right for them. He focused on the alleyway just ahead and a little nook where a gate was set back from the main fence.

Alfie spread his arms wide, herding Amy and Mrs Chieveley into this tiny piece of safety like an enthusiastic sheepdog.

They just got into the shelter as the tearing noise turned into a massive boom, the world shook like the skin of a bass drum, and a blast of hot air rushed past them.

Alfie shoved his hands over his ears and ducked his head down, thinking this was it. The Variado was using its weapons on them! What else could it be?

Alfie thought about his family, that last kiss from his mum, his dad's smile, the goodnight hug from Lizzie. He wished that things had turned out differently. Maybe he should have asked for help? Would they have believed him?

He was so busy blaming himself for everything having turned out so badly, that it took him a while to realize that they hadn't.

The noise didn't exactly stop, it just got quieter. Rather than a big roaring, explosive noise it was now more like popcorn being made. There were dull thuds and loud bangs, not something exploding, but things falling from the sky.

As Alfie poked his head out of their little nook to look up the alley, a large chunk of something metallic dropped right in his view with a clang.

'What *happened*?' Amy asked.

The ringing in Alfie's ears was so loud he could hardly hear her. He shook his head to tell her he didn't know, stepping out of the shelter of the nook to get a better view. He looked over the debris that had fallen in his path; the metal was bumpy almost like reptile skin. It wasn't like anything he'd seen before.

All the noise and shaking from the explosion had made his head foggy, but Alfie was starting to get an idea of what had happened. He didn't think the Variado had waited long before it had opened the crate. Now he knew what happened when frogs farted fire in a spaceship.

Alfie took a few steps back up the alley, countering the dizzy feeling by putting out a hand to touch the wall.

It was only when he got to the end and could see Parker's Field that he knew he was right. There was a lot of debris there. A spaceship's worth.

Amy appeared behind him. 'Oh wow,' she whispered. 'We blew it up. We blew that alien up!'

Alfie nodded, he could taste something bitter at the

back of his throat, like he was going to be sick. He'd killed something. Alright, it was an evil alien that wanted to steal from him, but even so, dead was dead. He didn't like that feeling at all.

'We did it, Alfie!' Amy said, clapping him on the back. 'We did it!'

Alfie just nodded again, staring out at the smoking wreckage of an alien spacecraft. Perhaps this wasn't the perfect solution after all.

How were they going to explain this? Someone must have called the police or the fire brigade with all that noise.

Just as he had that thought, he felt a vibration from his pocket. The key! He quickly pulled it out and said, 'Mr Monk?'

The computer's voice came loud and clear from the key.

'Alfie Slider, I have been monitoring your location. My sensors detected an explosion that destroyed the Variado's craft. The debris must not fall into human hands. It may be useful for repairing my systems. I will transport it to the *Monkesto* cargo bay.'

Alfie blinked, it was still hard to think and he wasn't quite following what the computer was saying.

Mr Monk's voice carried on, 'It is likely this will seriously drain my power, and I will need time to recharge. You will be unable to return to the *Monkesto* until my power reserves have been restored.'

Alfie was stunned. The day had gone just how he had planned it, but it hadn't turned out how he'd expected it at all.

'Yeah, sure,' he muttered absently. He couldn't think about what Mr Monk had said just yet. There was something he needed to say to the computer, though.

'We killed the Variado.'

'Sensors indicate the Variado's ship engaged an emergency protocol. All life forms were transported to an escape pod that is currently on a course out of your system and towards the Variado home world,' and as if Mr Monk realized Alfie wasn't quite operating at his usual level it added, 'The Variado, and the frogs, will live.'

Silence fell from the remote control then, and objects in front of Alfie began to disappear in the familiar rush of air and static that came with the *Monkesto*'s transport system.

Amy came alongside Alfie and gave him a quick hug.

'We did it!' she said, again, before letting him go and running back down the alley.

Alfie guessed she was going to check on Mrs Chieveley. He could only stand and stare as Mr Monk recycled the alien spaceship. It was over.

Thirty-four

Later that night, Alfie sat on the sofa between his parents, eating a bowl of cereal. Lizzie had gone to bed, and he was happy just to be where he was. Safe. Everyone was safe.

They'd taken Mrs Chieveley home and phoned her daughter so she could come and take care of the old lady. Amy had told her that Mrs Chieveley must have had a fall. Mrs Chieveley didn't remember much, so that had worked out alright.

Taking a last mouthful of cereal, Alfie put the bowl on the table and leaned back, making himself comfortable. Dad was watching TV, Mum was reading and it was all spectacularly, wonderfully, normal.

Alfie smiled, happy, resting his head on his mum's arm and watching the TV. It only took him a moment to realize that the news article was talking about the explosion.

The presenter was talking about the many reports of a loud noise over the village today. Their expert was suggesting that the RAF had been testing some kind of stealth aircraft and had dropped dangerously low.

A local man was talking about how he'd seen an explosion over Parker's Field, but the reporter made it clear no one believed him. There had been no debris found. Concerns were raised for future safety but without any evidence no one could really do anything.

The news soon moved on to talking about a politician opening a new part of the hospital. Boring!

Alfie let out a big sigh, and Mum looked down at him and slipped an arm around his shoulders.

'Penny for your thoughts?'

'I was just thinking about my story,' Alfie said. 'I think I've finished the first part. The bad guy has been defeated, but I don't know what the hero should do next.'

'Hmmm,' Mum thought about it. 'If the bad guy is gone, is there another threat or a problem for the hero to deal with, or is it just the end?'

'A problem,' Alfie agreed, 'Yes, there is a problem. The ship is still stuck, it needs to be repaired but…I don't know how I…the main character…could learn how to do that?'

'The data banks won't help?' Mum asked. 'Even if you could just repair the comms and get a signal off to the owners?'

A fizzing sensation in Alfie's head started, and he realized Mum was right. That was a great idea! If he could work out how to repair the communications system and get a signal off to the Skolto Service, they would deal with the rest! Then his stomach sank as he realized that meant they'd probably also collect the *Monkesto*. Mr Monk had been pretty clear that humans weren't ready to learn about alien technology yet.

'Maybe,' he said, sighing again. 'It doesn't matter for

now. Until the power reserves are back up, I can't get to the ship to ask Mr Monk.' Realizing what he'd said, Alfie tensed. Had he given the game away?

Mum chuckled, 'Oh, you really have got into this story, haven't you! You sound like you believe it yourself, and that's a brilliant first step to convincing other people.'

Alfie relaxed, nodding, and snuggling in alongside his mum. He had some time off. Until the *Monkesto*'s batteries were recharged he was stuck with normality and right now, normality seemed like a great idea.

Alfie knew whatever happened he was going to have to do the right thing, when the time came. For now though, he was going to make the most of it.

Thirty-five

It wasn't until the next day that Alfie started to wonder how long it would take the *Monkesto* to recharge. He realized that he didn't really know much about the ship at all. Where did it get its power from? It couldn't be fuel. It was stuck in another dimension and had no way to get more fuel so it must recharge itself somehow. Maybe it was wind or solar power? Aliens would be smart enough to use renewable energy, right? Solar wind power? That sounded sci-fi enough to be right.

In the early days, Alfie wasn't too worried about getting back. Life had been really intense since he'd found the key, and it was good to have a break. He was glad for the time to just be a normal kid again. He played computer games, and even enjoyed being back in school, especially the day that Omar came back and asked them all to sign his cast.

Amy asked him every day if he'd heard anything from Mr Monk, and she always looked disappointed when he said no.

Then the days stretched into a week, which became two, and Alfie started to worry, just a bit. Had the *Monkesto* repaired itself with the parts from the Variado's ship? Or had Mr Monk just decided to lock him out?

The cargo would be a lot safer if no one could get to it. Alfie would be a lot safer if the key didn't work. Maybe Mr Monk had decided that the best thing to do was just lock Alfie out. It made sense, and that's why Alfie couldn't quite get the idea out of his head.

Or maybe the Skolto Service had turned up and found the ship using scanners or something, and they'd just taken it away. There were so many possibilities in this big universe and Alfie didn't even know what was possible.

Every time he passed the knothole, at least twice a day, Alfie tried the key hoping that something would happen. Nothing did. It didn't vibrate, or let him hear Mr Monk's voice. When Alfie talked into it, he got no reply. It just wasn't working and Alfie had a horrible feeling it would never work again.

As much as Alfie was glad to be back to normal, he didn't want the story to end like that. He didn't want to just get left behind.

Then, one day as he was sitting in class, reading quietly, the key vibrated in his pocket. It pulsed out three short bursts, and then stopped. A few seconds later it repeated the rhythm again. Alfie felt like a house that had been instantly decorated for Christmas! He was shining with excitement.

Alfie looked over and saw Amy looking at him; she didn't have to ask the question he could read it on her face. He grinned broadly and gave her a big thumbs-up.

Their adventure wasn't over. The *Monkesto* was there, waiting for him to explore. He had to try and work out how to repair the ship and how to send a message off to aliens to tell them where it was. He had to make sure no more bad guys came and tried to take it for themselves. Oh no, Alfie's adventure wasn't over. It had only just begun!

Acknowledgements

With special thanks to: Patrick, Sally, Amy, Steve, Danny, Linda, Caroline, John, Jen (BFF), and everyone at York Writers for their constant support and encouragement. I couldn't have done it without you.

A huge thank you to the best beta readers anyone could ask for: Monique, Nicole, Nancy Mae, Ayda and, last but by no means least, my number one fan, Joseph. Thank you for showing me that children love Alfie Slider as much as I do.

Alfie's Next Adventure

Alfie Slider and the Frozen Prince

All Alfie Slider has to do is keep the *Monkesto* secret and safe, until the Skolto Service reply to his message. Simple, right? But then someone's elbow hits a big red button and Alfie and his friends get pulled into an interplanetary conflict. Does Alfie have what it takes to lead his team into a different world?

Link to the Monkesto

Thank you for reading *Alfie Slider vs the Shape Shifter*, I hope you enjoyed it!

Let others know what you thought about the book, by leaving a review on Amazon and Goodreads.

You can find Alfie Slider news and more here:

www.alfieslider.co.uk
Facebook.com/alfieslider
Twitter: @alfieslider